Welc...

Just when I th...

Now that the plant has fired that creepy guy, Vince, I figured I could relax and stop worrying about being caught. Then this foreign exchange student, Veronique, is assigned to stay with us. Great! Now I have to worry about a stranger catching me at an awkward moment, like when I'm glowing or morphing. Let me explain. . . .

I'm Alex Mack. I was just another average kid until my first day of junior high.

One minute I'm walking home from school—the next there's a *crash!* A truck from the Paradise Valley Chemical plant overturns in front of me, and I'm drenched in some weird chemical.

And since then—well, nothing's been the same. I can move objects with my mind, shoot electrical charges through my fingertips, and morph into a liquid shape . . . which is handy when I get in a tight spot!

My best friend, Ray, thinks it's cool—and my sister, Annie, thinks I'm a science project.

They're the only two people who know about my new powers. I can't let anyone else find out—not even my parents—because I know the chemical plant wants to find me and turn me into some experiment.

But you know something? I guess I'm not so average anymore!

The Secret World of Alex Mack™

Alex, You're Glowing!
Bet You Can't!
Bad News Babysitting!
Witch Hunt!
Mistaken Identity!
Cleanup Catastrophe!
Take a Hike!
Go for the Gold!
Poison in Paradise!
Zappy Holidays! (Super Edition)
Junkyard Jitters!
Frozen Stiff!
I Spy!
High Flyer!
Milady Alex!
Father-Daughter Disaster!
Bonjour, Alex!
Close Encounters!

Available from MINSTREL Books

NICKELODEON®

the secret world of

ALEX MACK™

I Spy!

John Peel

A MINSTREL®
BOOK

Published by POCKET BOOKS
New York London Toronto Sydney Tokyo Singapore

A MINSTREL PAPERBACK *Original*

 A Minstrel Book published by
POCKET BOOKS, a division of Simon & Schuster Inc.
1230 Avenue of the Americas, New York, NY 10020

Copyright © 1997 by Viacom International Inc., and RHI Entertainment, Inc. All rights reserved. Based on the Nickelodeon series entitled "The Secret World of Alex Mack."

ISBN: 0-671-00356-9

First Minstrel Books printing March 1997

10   9   8   7   6   5   4   3   2

NICKELODEON and all related titles, logos and characters are trademarks of Viacom International, Inc.

A MINSTREL BOOK and colophon are registered trademarks of Simon & Schuster Inc.

Cover photography by Thomas Queally

Printed in the U.S.A.

This is for Meagan and Lauren Finnegan

I Spy!

CHAPTER 1

"I am a disaster magnet!" Alex Mack exclaimed, perhaps a little too dramatically. Her outflung hand sent the rest of the box of corn flakes to the kitchen floor, to join the mess. "Oh, rats." She flicked her long hair out of her eyes and studied the soggy pile of milk and cereal.

"No, you're not," her older sister, Annie, replied brightly. "You're just inattentive."

Alex scowled. "Is that supposed to make me feel better?" she asked.

"No," Annie answered. "It's supposed to make you pay attention to what you're doing, instead of walking around in a fog and blaming everything that happens to you on fate or whatever your chosen object of blame for the day is." She sighed.

Shaking her head, Alex stared at the mess. "It's my age," she said. "I can't help it."

"There you go again," Annie said, exasperated. "Now you're blaming your age! Alex, grow up and accept responsibility for your own mistakes. And clean up that mess."

Alex started to raise her hand. Knowing what that meant, Annie grabbed her wrist. "Alex! For pete's sake! Not that way! Mom will be here any second, and if she saw you . . ." She didn't have to finish the sentence. Both of them knew what that meant.

On her way home from school one afternoon just over two years earlier, Alex had narrowly missed being hit by a truck. The driver, a less than bright individual named Dave, had swerved in time to miss her, but had spilled the contents of a barrel of top-secret chemical over Alex. The chemical—a new synthetic code-named GC-161—had soaked her, and then soaked into her, leaving her with some *very* curious side effects.

Alex was now super-powered, in an odd sort of way. She could use her mind to move objects; she could produce electrical zaps from her fingertips; weirdest of all, she could morph from a human being into a puddle of something that looked like water.

Not daring to report the accident, Alex had to hide her powers from everyone but her older sister, Annie, and her best friend, Ray Alvarado. Annie—a certified genius—was studying her sister to try and understand the strange effects of GC-161, and to make sure that there were no long-term ill effects on Alex. Ray simply thought that Alex was cool, and helped to keep her secret. That was only one of the reasons why he was Alex's best friend.

Nobody else knew about Alex's powers. Not her parents—Mr. and Mrs. Mack were terrific parents, but Alex and Annie knew that their first reaction would have been to panic and have Alex checked out professionally, spilling the beans about Alex's powers and making a human guinea pig of the Mack's youngest daughter. And especially not Danielle Atron, the head of Paradise Valley Chemical, who had developed GC-161. Ms. Atron was a scheming, self-centered, and cold creature who would have gladly dissected Alex as part of her own research into GC-161, which she was convinced would make her wealthy beyond her wildest dreams.

So Alex had to keep her mysterious powers hidden, something she had a tendency to forget from time to time. Like now. "But it'll take forever the normal way," Alex protested.

"Alex!" Annie warned.

"Oh, all right." Fetching the broom and pan, Alex started cleaning up.

Bustling into the kitchen, staring around the room, her mother said, "Have you seen my homework, Annie? I know I left it somewhere."

"In the den, Mom," Annie replied. She was used to keeping track of her mother's papers. Mrs. Mack had recently quit her job in public relations to return to college. It was tough having three of the four members of the Mack home all studying at once.

"Right," Mrs. Mack smiled brightly. "Okay, everything under control here?"

"Everything's just fine, Mom," Alex grumbled, mopping up the milk. "I love cleaning the kitchen floor."

Mrs. Mack blinked. "Well, now's not the time to try and be helpful, Alex. It's time to get ready for school. Ray's going to be here any moment, you know. I don't want you to think I don't appreciate your help, dear, but there's a time and place for everything."

Alex raised her eyes and sighed.

As she trudged down the block with Ray, Alex asked him, "Do you think I'm a klutz?"

Ray raised his eyebrows and stared at her.

"You, a klutz? No way. You're just having a bad day, that's all. You'll be better tomorrow."

"Thanks, Ray," Alex replied with a sigh. "That really makes me feel better."

"Hey, come on!" Ray protested with a wide grin. "I was just joking. Alex, what's with you today?"

"I don't know," Alex admitted. "I just feel sort of . . . unlucky today. Like there's a cloud of doom hovering over me, waiting to zap me when I'm not looking."

"That's no cloud of doom," Ray assured her. "It's just Robyn. Look."

Alex raised her eyes and saw her other two best friends waving to them from across the road. She had to chuckle at Ray's description of Robyn. The red-haired girl was a wonderful person, but she did tend to look on the bleak side of things. Standing with her was Nicole, who tended to be very serious, very intense, and fiercely loyal. Alex often wished she could tell the two of them about her abilities, but she knew that it would only lead to trouble. She hated keeping secrets from them, but this was one they were better off not knowing. She forgot about her problems, and the four of them chattered away about nothing important all the way to school.

During third period, she had another accident. It was music, and the teacher, Miss Henderson, was talking about musical appreciation. Alex wasn't paying too close attention, because music to her was what she listened to on her stereo or Walkman. Classical music didn't cut it for her. Miss Henderson was talking about the instruments of the orchestra. Alex wished she'd talk about more relevant stuff, like electric guitars and synthesizers.

Then a fly started to buzz about her. Alex grimaced and tried to ignore it. But for some reason, the fly found her fascinating and refused to leave. Finally Alex smacked at it with her hand.

"Oh, very good, Alex," Miss Henderson said brightly. "I have to confess that I never expected you to volunteer, but I'm very glad that you have."

"Huh?" Alex forgot all about the fly and stared at the teacher, who was beaming at her. She tried to recall what Miss Henderson had exactly been saying, but it was no good. She didn't dare say that she hadn't *really* volunteered for anything, because Miss Henderson was already taking down the names of other people who were volunteering. Instead she leaned over to Ray. "What did I just volunteer for?" she whispered.

Ray grinned. "You don't know?" he whispered back. "Alex, you should have been paying attention."

"I *tried*." Alex claimed, exaggerating slightly. "But I was distracted. What am I in for now?"

"You just volunteered to learn how to play a musical instrument," Ray answered. "To foster classical-music appreciation."

Alex stared at him in horror. *Music* lessons? She winced. Her mother had tried to get Alex to take piano lessons when she was five. That had lasted for a lesson and a half before the teacher had told Mrs. Mack that Alex seemed to have been born with two left hands. Now what had she done?

CHAPTER 2

"So you're my little niece?" Vince asked, staring harshly at the teenager who stood before him.

"Not so little," she replied, matching him glare for glare.

Abruptly Vince grinned. "You've got some of my steel in you," he said. "I like that. It shows character."

His niece now shared his grin. "We're a lot alike, Uncle Vince. I guess that's why my folks named me after you."

Vince nodded. "Vincenza," he said.

She winced. "Puh-leese! Call me Vincie."

"Okay, Vincie," Vince agreed. "It does sound a lot better." He glanced down again at the letter from his kid brother he'd been reading when his niece had arrived. "According to this, you've managed to get yourself into a certain amount of . . . trouble."

Vincie sighed and raised her eyes to the ceiling. "It wasn't anything, really."

Vince studied his niece carefully. She was tall, almost as tall as he was, and slim. But he could see that she had firm muscles—obviously a very good athlete. She wasn't the let's-visit-the-mindless-mall-type, that was for sure. Another good mark in her favor. And she was quite attractive, too. Like him, she sported her blond hair very closely cropped. And she had his piercing eyes, too. They might almost be father and daughter, not uncle and niece. Vince wondered . . . might it actually be . . . *nice* to have a child?

He instantly dismissed the thought. What a foolish thing to consider. He was a security officer first and foremost, and probably the best in the business. Danger was his job and his reward. It was what he lived to combat. There was no room in his life for personal entanglements. They only slowed you down, held you back, and made you worry at the wrong moment. Still, he *had* agreed to look after Vincie for a while, to whip her into shape for his wimpy brother. And he had another purpose, of course. . . .

"Nothing really?" he asked Vincie. "According to your father, you were expelled from your last school for beating up three boys."

"Four, actually," Vincie admitted. "But the fourth refused to admit I'd given him the black eye, so I was let off on that one."

"Four boys," Vince corrected himself. "And the school before that expelled you for blowing up their chemistry laboratory."

"Only *half* of it," Vincie complained. "Well, the lesson was so boring and fundamental, and I'd always wanted to make TNT—"

"In a crowded classroom?" Vince growled. "Somebody might have been hurt. Besides, it's always best to wait until no one else is around to steal your ideas, you idiot. Like I did."

Vincie stared at him, something akin to hero worship in her eyes. "You made TNT at school?"

"Yeah. But I wasn't dumb enough to get caught." Vince sighed. "Listen, Vincie, your father's about given up on you. He calls you a wild savage brat—"

Vincie looked surprised. "That's the nicest thing he's ever said about me."

"Yeah, well, that's in the first paragraph. He gets worse toward the end of the letter. Anyway, the point is, he's sent you here to stay with me for a while to see if I can get you to settle down for a while." He waved the letter under her nose.

"And if that doesn't work, he's sending you to boot camp in Nome, Alaska."

Vincie managed a winning smile. "I'll be good, Uncle Vince. I promise."

"Like I'm supposed to *believe* that?" Vince asked her, incredulously. "I know I don't have kids, but I'm not dumb. You *will* behave, because the alternative is Alaska. In winter. In the snow."

"I *like* snow."

"Me, too," Vince agreed. "But not for breakfast. *That's* the sort of thing you'll get in boot camp, trust me."

Vincie's grin started to fade slightly. "Well, my folks seem to think that you can set me straight. I just don't happen to think I *need* setting straight."

With a snort, Vince tossed the letter down on his desk. "Your father's a good kid," he said. "But he was always a bit of a wimp. So *you* don't think you need setting straight, huh?" He glowered at her. "You're not old enough to have such opinions, kid."

"I am, too," Vincie snapped back. "I'm fifteen."

"Fifteen's *nothing*," Vince insisted. "Unless . . ."

She bit the bait. "Unless *what?*"

"Unless you're smart," he told her. "I knew what I wanted when I was twelve, and I worked real hard to get there. Okay, it meant I wasn't popular in school, but I didn't care about that. I always knew I had a career in industrial espionage ahead of me. I practiced by bugging the classrooms and feeding information to the teachers. Then, just to show I wasn't prejudiced, I bugged the staff room and fed test questions to the other kids. And I never got caught doing it. That's why I'm one of the greatest security officers in the field today."

Vincie gave a smug grin. "And why Danielle Atron fired you?"

That wiped the nostalgic smile from Vince's face. "Who told you that?"

Vincie pulled something from her bag and held it up. It was a photocopy of a memo on the Paradise Valley Chemical letterhead. "You're not the only one in the family that can find things out, you know."

The sight of his dismissal notice brought a dark mood over Vince. "My one and only failure," he growled. "In all my years of industrial espionage, my only failure. The GC-161—" He pulled himself together. "Anyway, I now run my own private security business, so this was a career move, not a firing."

"Yeah, sure, whatever," Vincie agreed. "Does that mean you're not interested in going back to work for Miss Atron?'' She finally put down her duffel bag and school backpack.

"No," Vince admitted. "I'd love a chance to wipe my slate clean again. To recover my perfect record. To capture that kid and to have Miss Atron apologize for . . ." His voice trailed off. "I'm starting to get an idea."

"Is it a good one?" Vincie asked excitedly. "Can I be a part of it?"

"A part of it?" Vince slapped her on the shoulder. "A *major* part of it. And, no, it's not a *good* idea. It's a *great* idea. . . ." He thought it through for a moment. "You're supposed to enroll in Danielle Atron Junior High today," he explained. "Well, you will. But not as Vincie. You're going to be a foreign exchange student instead. We need you to seem authentic. Can you actually speak any foreign languages?"

"Not as such," Vincie answered. "But I can do a pretty good fake French accent. *Vive la France! J'aime escargots.*"

"Well, there's no need to go *that* far," Vince replied. "Snails are only so-so survival food. You're not supposed to *enjoy* them. But I guess that'll have to do. If anyone asks you to speak any real French, tell them you've got to practice your English. Make it more real by making some silly mistakes with English, okay?"

"Got it," Vincie said excitedly. "But I've a feeling I'm going to enjoy this. So, what is it that you want me to do?"

"Espionage," Vince answered. "You're going to be my undercover spy. Together, we'll discover who the GC-161 kid is, and then inform Danielle Atron. If you've got one tenth of my talent, by the end of the week, you'll have your first victory, and I'll have my old job back. We've got a little bit of work to do on you, and then we'll introduce the world to the new you. . . ."

"It's no good, Ray," Alex said helplessly. "The more I try to be careful, the worse things seem to get."

"You're worrying too much about it, Alex," Ray replied, helping her to pick her books up off the floor. The custodian had managed to fix her lock—with muttered comments about teenage vandals—but when Alex had opened her locker, everything in it had behaved like it was going over Niagara Falls. She and Ray were cramming them back.

"Alex!" Robyn called down the hallway. "What are you doing, standing there asleep like that? Miss Henderson's looking for you. Did you forget about the music-appreciation thingy?"

Music appreciation! Alex jolted back to reality

as serenity gave way to panic. It had completely passed out of her mind. "Oh, gosh," she muttered. "I'd better get moving." She glanced at Robyn. "What did you get stuck with?"

Robyn held up a small case. "This."

Frowning, Alex tried to figure it out. "What's in something that small?" she asked. "A violin for a mouse?"

"It's a triangle," Robyn explained. "One note. Boring. It's like Miss Henderson is saying that I'm too dumb or something to learn to play anything else. If you ask me, it's demeaning."

"Maybe," Ray agreed. "But at least you don't have pages of music to memorize, do you?"

Robyn actually brightened at that thought. "That's true," she agreed. She waved as Alex shot down the corridor. "See you."

Alex finally made it to the music annex. She hurried into the instrument room, puffing hard. Miss Henderson glanced up from the list she was going over on her desk.

"Sorry I'm late," Alex apologized. Then she stared hopefully at the bare shelves. "Oh, am I too late to be assigned an instrument?" She could hope, at least! Maybe, at last, something would go right today.

"Not at all, Alex," the teacher answered, dashing her hopes. "Though you are too late to be able to make a choice. You'll have to take the only instrument I've got left." She reached behind her desk and pulled out a massive long case. "The music's in there with it, along with the instruction book."

Alex took the heavy case. She was going to get exhausted just carrying this home. "What is it?" she asked, gasping. "A cannon?"

"Not quite," the music teacher answered. "It's a trombone. Now, try and practice at least an hour tonight. Then, after school tomorrow, I'll see what you've learned and give you a few pointers."

Alex eyed the case with some trepidation. "Uh, Miss Henderson," she asked hesitantly. "What if I don't get the hang of it?"

"Then we'll see if we can switch you to another instrument," the teacher replied. "This is just to see if you can get used to the instrument. We don't expect you to be able to play it properly without the twice-weekly lesson schedule I'm drawing up. Of course, to be able to switch, we'll have to find another pupil who'll be willing to switch with you." She smiled encouragingly. "Don't worry, Alex. This isn't supposed to be some kind of punishment. I want you to enjoy what you're doing. We can't *force* you to enjoy music—it has to be a natural outspringing. If you *really* don't like this, of course I'll let you out. But I want you to promise me that you will at least *try* to see if there's any musical ability inside of you. Okay?"

Alex nodded. "Okay," she agreed. Privately, though, she was pretty certain that this was going to be another embarrassing failure for her. Picking up the heavy case again, she left the music office and made her way back to the lockers.

Ray and Robyn were still there, and now Nicole had joined them. They glanced sympathetically at Alex as she approached.

"What did you get stuck with?" Robyn asked, eyeing the case.

"It's a trombone," Alex answered. "Though from the weight of it, I'd say seventy-six trombones was more like it."

"Tough," Nicole said, and sighed. "If you ask me, this so-called music appreciation is actually a plot to get us to hate music. And that's a good thing when you think about it."

"How can that be a good thing?" Ray asked, puzzled. "Me, I love music. It's almost my whole life." He played an air sax as he spoke.

"Yes, for you," Nicole agreed. "But look at what adults do to kids who are *really* gifted. Beethoven's father made him practice hours a day and once slammed his son's hands in a piano for playing the wrong note. Mozart was forced on a concert tour when he was seven. As for Haydn, he was in a boy's choir until his voice broke, and then he was thrown out into the streets, penniless, to fend for himself. It's all exploitation, if you ask me."

"I hardly think they're going to find another Mozart hiding out at Danielle Atron Junior High," Alex objected. "So I wouldn't worry about it."

Robyn eyed her case skeptically. "Do you think I'm going to get blisters playing this? I have very sensitive skin, you know. It goes with red hair, sensitive skin."

"I think I'm going to strain a muscle," Alex complained. "And that's even before I play a note." They pushed through the doors and out into the bright afternoon sunshine.

"Want me to carry your case?" Ray offered.

"Thanks, but no," Alex replied. "It's my job, I guess. On the other hand, I may accept before we get home. Why don't they make wheels for these things?"

"That," Robyn answered, "would be too easy. You're supposed to suffer for your art."

"I'm suffering," Alex assured her. "And I don't even *have* any art!"

CHAPTER 3

Vince studied his niece with a large grin of triumph. "You're looking good," he told her. "But there's just one thing missing."

"What?" Vincie glanced down at her very perky skirt and flounced blouse with disgust. "Don't I look just cute enough to die for?" She groaned. "You know, Uncle, I'm going to really *suffer* wearing these tacky clothes."

"You have to look authentic," Vince informed her. "The first rule of a successful spy is that you have to *live* your role."

"I guess," Vincie agreed. "And I *do* want to be a success. You'll be proud of me, you just wait and see."

"You know, I do believe you might be right,"

Vince answered. "You're a girl after my own heart. If I had one." He studied her critically again, then snapped his fingers. "Got it." He went into the next room and emerged a few moments later carrying a long blond wig. "Put this on."

"Yech," Vincie complained. "Do I have to? It must weigh pounds."

"*Kilos*," Vince corrected her. "They're on the metric system in France, remember? You have to watch things like that."

"Right." With a sigh, Vincie took the wig and put it on. "It *does* weigh kilos."

"But it tops off the disguise," Vince informed her. "With your short hair, somebody might have guessed you were related to me. Now you look completely different. Besides, good spies always wear disguises."

That cheered her up. "Right, they do, don't they?" She studied her image in a full-length mirror. "It looks so unlike *me*," she said with approval. "Nobody would normally catch me dead wearing stuff like this. *C'est magnifique, n'est-ce pas?*"

"I'll say," Vince agreed. "That's the easy part, though." He pointed to a pile of magazines and books. "You'd better start studying those, to catch up on what every good French girl should know. Meanwhile, I'm going to have to arrange for somewhere for you to stay."

"Huh?" Vincie looked disappointed. "I thought I was going to stay here with you."

"As Vincie, you were," Vince agreed. "But as your new identity, Veronique Deschamps, you couldn't. You're supposed to be an exchange student whose host family had a crisis. You'll have to stay with a local family, and only come here to report to me. And from now on, you're *Veronique* to everyone, including me." He frowned as he considered the housing problem. "Come with me," he said, leading her into his supply room.

Vincie's eyes opened wide as she surveyed the stacked shelves of his gadgets and gizmos. "Wow! Talk about Santa's workshop!" She picked up a miniature camera disguised as a pen. "This stuff's really neat. Do I get to play with it all?"

Grabbing the pen from her hand, Vince put it back on its shelf. "These things aren't toys," he answered sternly. "You'll be issued whatever I think will help you with your mission. Right now, the main thing's over here." He led her to a desk, where he had a laptop computer linked into his own computer. Tapping in commands, he brought up the main screen. "I've fed in the names, addresses, and whatever we know of every kid in the area. It's going to be your job to check them all out. There's a file for each kid. All we know is that probably one of the brats from the junior high school is the GC-161 kid. It might be one of the other schools, though, so don't limit yourself. The only eyewitness is basically a rock on legs, and he's no help. You've got to find out what you can on these kids, and enter it all in here."

"Got it," Vincie agreed. "Do I get to use a lot of your fun stuff?"

"I haven't decided, yet," Vince answered. "Your best tools as a spy are your eyes and ears," he added. "All these little toys are a help, but they can't substitute for your personal observation and using your brain. As soon as I know you can do that, then I'll see about issuing you some tools to go with them."

"Okay, I suppose," Vincie agreed with regret.

"Right." Vince unplugged the laptop and handed it to her. Then he went to his main computer and accessed the files. "We need to get you into a good average family. One with a kid about your age, so you'll have someone to hang around with. It had better be a girl, so she can introduce you to people." As he spoke, he was typing in a list of commands. "Someone who works for the chemical plant might be a plus, but not one I had much to do with from day to day. We wouldn't want to risk someone getting suspicious of you."

A list of ten names came up on the screen. "Any of these would be possible," he mused, glancing down the list. "Beck, Thompson, Mack . . ." He paused. "Mack. That name rings a bell." He tapped in the code, and the information sprang up. "Ah, George Mack . . . I remember him. He's one of the team assigned to investigate the properties of GC-161." Vince smiled. "He'd be perfect. As well as checking on the kids, you could look around and see if he's discovered anything about the chemical that might be useful to know. Talk about killing two birds with one stone."

"You want me to spy on him, too?" Vincie asked. "Cool! I'm starting to really like working with you, Uncle Vince."

"Good. Right, I'll give them a call later tonight, and set things up with them. I'm sure they won't turn down aiding a poor stranded foreign girl in distress. And once you're inside their house, you can start hunting for the GC-161 kid. And the first person you can check out is . . . Alex Mack."

Alex sat in the garage, staring at the instructions she had propped up on one of Annie's test-tube racks and holding the trombone awkwardly. "It won't hold still," she complained. "It must be broken."

Patiently, Ray showed her again how to hold it. "That part's called the slide," he explained. "It's *supposed* to move. That's how you control the sound it makes."

"Oh." Alex glared at the instrument. "Seems like a stupid arrangement to me."

"Trust me, it works," Ray insisted. "Okay, now you pucker up your lips and then blow into the mouthpiece. It's easy."

"Pucker up my lips?" Alex repeated. "This is supposed to be *fun?*"

"Pretend you're kissing it," Ray suggested.

Even that idea didn't cheer Alex up. "I can assure you, Ray, that kissing somebody and sticking my lips onto this metal monster are *very* different experiences. Well, at least I *hope* they would be."

"Just try it, Alex," Ray requested.

Taking a deep breath, Alex stuck her lips against the mouthpiece and blew hard.

A horrible wail came from the other end of the instrument. "It sounds like a warthog having its teeth extracted without novocaine," she complained.

"Yeah, but that was pretty good for a first

try," Ray said encouragingly. "It's just that the note was a bit flat. Let's try again."

With a sigh, Alex did so. The second note didn't sound any healthier than the first, but Ray persevered. In about twenty minutes, Alex was at least getting closer to a musical note. She was also getting very sore lips and amazingly frustrated.

"I *really* hate this instrument, Ray," she said. "There's no marks where the slide should go, and no buttons or keys or anything to press or play. It's all guesswork, if you ask me."

Ray shook his head. "Getting the hang of any instrument isn't easy, Alex. It takes practice and perseverance."

"So *that's* what you're up to, Alex, playing a trombone?" Annie commented as she entered the garage. "I thought the house was haunted."

"Very funny," Alex muttered. "I suppose *you* can play one of these in your sleep?"

"Maybe," her sister replied. "But not while I'm awake." She thought for a moment. "Actually, I've never tried. But music is based on mathematical progression, you know, so maybe I'd be pretty good at it."

"You probably would be," Alex answered with a sigh.

Annie smiled. "Don't give up so easily, Alex,"

she said encouragingly. "You never know, you may actually have a natural aptitude for the trombone. Come on, I'll stay and encourage you for a while."

Alex appreciated her sister's comfort. "Thanks." She gripped the trombone tightly again. Pressing her lips against it, she blew hard into the mouthpiece.

A long, low, reasonably musical note issued out of the trombone, to Alex's amazement. This feeling didn't last long, because another immediately took over.

A surging tingle passed right through her body, and the next thing she knew, Alex was a molten puddle of liquid on the floor of the garage.

"Alex!" she heard her sister scream in that strange dislocated voice she always heard in this state. Lacking ears, she tended to absorb sound through her whole body while morphed. "This is no time to play around."

Concentrating hard, Alex managed to reform herself. She stood there, glaring at the trombone, which she held once again. "I wasn't playing, Annie," she answered. "Something just . . . happened. I don't know why. I simply morphed without willing it."

Annie stared at her in concern. "It just came over you for no reason?"

"There has to be a reason," Ray said, frowning. "Maybe it was the trombone somehow."

"How?" Annie asked practically. "She's been playing it for a while, and this didn't happen before."

"It was the low note," Alex guessed. "It sort of reverberated right through me. I'm sure that was it."

Ever practical, Annie said, "Well, let's test it and see. Play a high note."

"I'm lucky to play *any* note on this thing," Alex muttered, but she complied. A rather shaky squeaky note emerged. "Nothing."

"Okay." Annie had her notepad handy and was scribbling frantically. This would end up in her research notes at the end of the day. "Now try a low note again."

Alex did so, playing as close as she could to the note she'd managed last time.

Instantly the tingling flew through her again, and she was a ball of liquid on the floor again. Concentrating, she managed to regain her real shape. "Well, I guess that proves it," she said, staring in disgust at the trombone as Ray recovered it.

"Not quite," Annie turned to Ray. "You try

playing that same note, and let's see if it affects her."

Alex winced. "Annie, this whole thing is giving me the creeps. Can't we just stop?"

"Not until we have some scientific results," Annie insisted. "I'm sorry, Alex, but we have do to this thoroughly. Go ahead, Ray."

Ray nodded and blew. A low cool note emerged from the trombone, real music, not what Alex had been approximating. Alex felt a slight shiver, but nothing like before.

"Nothing," she reported. "It didn't have any effect on me."

Annie nodded in satisfaction. "So it only happens when *you* play the low note." She thought for a moment. "Must be something to do with the harmonic frequencies. Maybe they match your body's natural resonances, or something. I wonder if this happens with all instruments, or just the trombone? What we need is a sampling of other instruments so that we'll be able to determine their effect on your metabolism."

Alex winced at the thought of more testing. "Uh, Annie," she said. "I hate to break up a line of scientific thought once you've started. But I think you're missing the point here."

"I am?" Annie blinked and looked puzzled. "How so?"

Alex gestured at the trombone. "I'm supposed to play that thing at school, in front of at least Miss Henderson, if not the whole class. If I do so, I'm going to be exposed once I morph."

CHAPTER 4

Alex was still brooding over her problem at dinnertime. She had to get out of playing the trombone somehow. She supposed she could just tell Miss Henderson that she'd changed her mind about the whole music-appreciation thing, but she was rather reluctant to do that. It was too much like quitting, and Alex didn't want to be a quitter.

Because of her preoccupied state of mind, she almost dropped the glasses as she was helping set the table for dinner. A quick recovery saved her from sweeping up broken glass. She pulled herself together and tried to concentrate on the job at hand. The last thing she needed right now was to slip back into her walking-disaster mode.

Annie was tossing the salad, while Alex mixed up the dressing, when the phone rang. There was a chorus of "I'll get it!" But it was Mrs. Mack who actually made the catch and picked up the phone.

"Hello, Mack residence," she said brightly. "Um, yes, yes, it is." She listened with the phone hunched into her shoulder as she tried to use pot holders to reach into the oven. "Uh-huh."

Alex rushed to help. "I'll do this," she said, taking the pot holders. "And I'll be careful." Mrs. Mack nodded her thanks, relinquishing the baking dish to Alex. While her mother moved off to continue the conversation, Alex heaved the large dish from the oven and then carefully carried it through into the dining room and placed it on the waiting trivet.

Annie stared at it with scientific disdain. "What *is* that?" she asked.

"Don't ask me," Alex answered. "It's one of Mom's new vegetarian recipes."

Mr. Mack leaned over it, his nose wrinkling uncertainly. "It smells . . . interesting," he finally decided. "I'll get the vegetables." As he breezed back into the kitchen, they heard him ask, "Will you be much longer, Barbara? Dinner's ready."

Alex stared at the dish. "Another experimental

recipe. Between you and Mom, I feel like I've been trapped in a laboratory already."

Annie was just as unenthusiastic about the dish. Mrs. Mack meant well, but her vegetarian dishes were generally unmitigated disasters that even a starving mutt wouldn't eat. "This one might be better than most" was the most hope she could hold out.

"It's going to have to go a long way to be worse than that banana breadfruit pie," Alex commented. "Uh, there's no bananas in this, is there?"

"Hard to tell," Annie answered. "I could take it to the garage and dissect it if you like."

"Now, girls," their father said, emerging from the kitchen with a big dish filled with mixed vegetables, "there's no need to be so critical. Your mother is doing her best, and some of these recipes turn out really well."

Annie raised an eyebrow. "Statistically speaking," she observed, "we have a failure rate of around eighty-four percent."

Her father frowned at that thought, then brightened. "So there's at least a sixteen-percent chance of success," he commented, determined to look on the bright side. He glanced at the kitchen. "Are you about done, sweetheart?"

Alex heard her mother hang up the phone and then Mrs. Mack joined them at the table, looking rather distracted. "This looks interesting, Mom," she said cheerily. "What is it?"

"Hmm?" Her mother shook her head to refocus. "It's dinner, dear. Shall we start?" She helped herself to salad and then a big spoonful of the main course. The rest of the family took smaller experimental portions. Alex eyed her sample suspiciously, then started in on the salad.

"Who was that on the phone, dear?" Mr. Mack asked, also safely munching on his salad.

"It was somebody in the education department," Mrs. Mack announced. "Um . . . we're going to be having a visitor stay with us for a few weeks, it seems."

"What?" Annie asked, pausing with a slice of tomato inches from her mouth. "A *visitor?* Who?"

"Some stranded French girl, it seems," Mrs. Mack replied. "She was supposed to stay with relatives, but they came down with some contagious sickness while she was en route, and now the poor girl is stranded. Apparently the education department did some sort of compatibility test or something, and decided that we would be the perfect family to be her host while she's in Paradise Valley."

"Just like that?" Annie asked, obviously annoyed.

"Apparently." Mrs. Mack looked a little bemused. "They did explain it, but with all the noise of getting dinner ready, I didn't catch it all."

Mr. Mack frowned slightly. "I do rather think that we should have discussed this before saying yes," he complained mildly. "After all, this is going to affect the whole family."

Mrs. Mack shrugged. "Apparently she's arriving tomorrow, and they had to have an answer right away. After all, George, she *is* all alone, and she *is* stranded. I just thought about how we'd feel if it was Alex in that situation, and I know we'd want a kind family to take her in and look after her. So I couldn't really refuse, could I?"

Her husband looked slightly taken aback at this barrage of words, and he muttered, "No, I suppose not."

Alex pounced on the interesting part of the speech. "Does that mean I get to go to France in exchange?"

"No," her mother answered. "I'm afraid not."

"Mom," Annie said, more practically, "where's this girl going to stay? We don't have a guest room, and our room's already overflowing with the two of us and Alex's hat collection."

Mrs. Mack smiled. "We've got the pull-out couch," she said. "Veronique—that's her name—

can sleep on that. That's how we put Grandma up, after all."

"Well," Mr. Mack said finally, "that seems to settle that. It might be nice having a fresh face about the house for a couple of weeks, at any rate." He dug a large forkful of the main course up from his plate and swallowed it. "Say! This is actually very good!"

"Well, of course it is," his wife answered, frowning at him. "Did you think I would poison my family?"

"Not intentionally, Mom," Alex commented. She tried a smaller forkful of the stuff. To her amazement, her father was right. "Hey, this *is* good."

Annie stared at hers, unconvinced. "I'd still like a list of ingredients first—or a thorough analysis." Catching the hurt expression on her mother's face, she cracked a smile. "Just kidding." She started to eat her own.

"Well, just think," Mrs. Mack said brightly. "This time tomorrow, we'll have a foreign visitor sitting here at dinner with us. I wonder if she likes vegetarian food, too?"

The following morning didn't bring much relief for Alex. She tripped over the trombone case when she leaped out of bed, having overslept her alarm as usual. Then she dropped her English muffin as she was trying to rush breakfast. Finally she forgot the trombone case when she dashed out of the door, then had to run back for it when Ray reminded her about it.

"Another great day in the life of Alex Mack," she muttered breathlessly, rejoining Ray. "What am I going to do with this thing?"

"You've got to get rid of it," Ray said. "You certainly can't play it if it makes you morph."

"Yeah, I know that," Alex agreed. "But how do I get rid of it?"

"Get someone to swap with you," Ray suggested. "Here's a couple of likely victims now." He gestured across the street, where Robyn and Nicole were waiting for them. Both had their own music cases with them.

"Hey," Alex said, brightening up a little. "Maybe there's hope yet." She struggled to catch up with her girlfriends. "How's the music practice going?" she asked them.

"You know," Robyn said thoughtfully, "I really didn't think I was going to get into this musical-appreciation thing. It seemed just like another way for the teachers to oppress our spirits and browbeat us into submitting to their middle-class agenda."

Alex frowned as she tried to follow this. "But?" she prompted.

"Well, I played my triangle last night, and guess what?" Robyn smiled. "It was just *so* cool. Sort of a Zen thing. I think I'm really getting into this. I felt as if I were at one with the triangle and the note that emerged."

Though she wasn't entirely sure she followed what Robyn was saying, at least one thing was clear. "So you kind of liked it, huh?" No chance of a swap there. . . .

"It's fun," Robyn admitted. Then she added hastily, "But don't tell *everyone*. I have a reputation to live up to for depression."

Alex sighed. "How about you, Nicole?" she asked, without much hope.

"I hate this thing," Nicole answered frankly. "I couldn't even *touch* it."

"You couldn't," Alex asked, delighted. "Uh, I mean, why not? What's wrong?"

"It's the bow," Nicole explained. "I didn't realize that they use *horse hair* to make the bows. I mean, I'm all for musical appreciation and the arts, but not when it comes to cruelty to animals. I simply refuse to learn a musical instrument that involves torturing poor horses."

Ray scowled. "Cutting their hair isn't torturing them," he protested. Alex elbowed him in the ribs, warningly, and nodded at the trombone case. He realized that he'd almost blown the exchange for Alex. "Then again," he said hastily, "what do I know about how the horses feel about it? Personally, I hate the barber's myself."

"Exactly," said Nicole in satisfaction. "So I am going to see Miss Henderson this morning and *demand* a change of instrument."

"Oh, there's no need to do that, Nicole," Alex said generously. "I mean, I'd be more than happy to trade with you if you'd like. This trombone isn't cruel to anyone."

"Except the listeners when Alex plays it," Ray added, grinning.

"You'd trade?" Nicole asked happily. "Oh, thanks, Alex. You're a real friend."

As they exchanged cases, Alex grinned. "Think nothing of it, Nicole. You're doing *me* a favor taking that thing off my hands. I really can't get the hang of it." Another advantage to the violin, Alex reflected, was that it weighed a lot less than the trombone did! "We can just tell Miss Henderson about the trade later."

Feeling a lot cheerier now that her main problem was solved, Alex continued on the way to school brightly, chatting to her friends. At school, her locker behaved for once, and they reached their home room without incident.

Their teacher called for attention, and when she had it, she smiled and pointed to a new girl. "Class, this is Veronique Deschamps. She's a visiting exchange student from France who will be with us for a few weeks. I'm sure you'll all make her very welcome and help her to settle in. Ah, Alex, I believe she will be staying with your family. Perhaps it would be best if she sat next to you, so you could get to know each other better."

Alex had completely forgotten about the French girl. "Uh, right," she agreed, smiling at the stranger. "Hi, I'm Alex. It's nice to meet you."

"*Allo*," Veronique replied, shaking hands. "It is my pleasure to meet you. I 'ope we can be friends."

"I hope so, too," Alex answered. "Um, I'm afraid I don't know much French. I'm not too good with languages."

"That is fine," Veronique answered. "I am 'ere to make my English much better. So I prefer it to speak in your language. That way, I will learn faster."

"You sound pretty good to me," Ray commented. "Hi, I'm Ray Alvarado."

"He's my best friend," Alex explained.

"*Allo*, Ray," Veronique said. "Thank you for your condiment."

Alex frowned at this, then smiled. "I think you mean *compliment*."

Veronique smiled and nodded. "Ah, that is right. I do."

The bell rang for first class, and Alex led the girl off. For the rest of the morning, Veronique stayed close to her, paying careful attention to everything. She asked Alex the names of everyone that they met, and said *allo* to everyone to whom she was introduced. Alex couldn't help quite liking the young girl.

At lunchtime, Veronique took a laptop computer from her bag as they found a table. "I am going to 'ave to make some notes," she explained to Alex and Ray. "Or else I know I shall forget some things."

"I'll get you some lunch," Alex offered. "What do you like?"

"As I am in America now, I shall 'ave to eat American," Veronique replied. "Could I 'ave— how do you say it?—a burger?"

"Sure," Alex agreed.

"And French fries," the French girl added. "I adore French fries."

"No problem." Alex dumped her bag. "Come on, Ray."

Ray tagged along, looking puzzled. "That was kind of odd, don't you think?" he asked.

"What was kind of odd, Ray?" Alex asked, not following what he had said.

"Veronique asking for French fries."

Alex frowned at him as they got on the cafeteria line. "What's so odd about that?" she asked. "I love French fries, too. So do you. In fact, you usually steal some of mine."

"Yeah, but that's not what I mean." Ray looked puzzled. "She had problems pronouncing *burger*, but she got French fries the first time. And in France, they're not called French fries. I know because my dad went there once. He told me that all of the things *we* call French—like French fries, French horns, or French windows— *they* call *English.* So, why didn't Veronique ask for *English* fries?"

"Ray, what's gotten into you?" Alex asked. "Who cares why she called them French fries? Maybe she likes them so much she learned their name by heart." She gave him a slightly annoyed glance. "Lighten up, will you?"

"Maybe," Ray said, obviously unconvinced. "But there's just something about her. I can't put my finger on it, but . . ."

"Don't tell me you're prejudiced against the French?" Alex asked. "Ray, you are sometimes so paranoid that you make Robyn look almost normal."

"I guess," Ray agreed reluctantly. "Well, let's do what I hope you don't do with that tray—drop it."

They both got their lunches and headed back to join Veronique. The French girl had just finished her notes and clipped the laptop shut. "That looks great," she said happily, and the three of them started in on their lunch.

"So, how do you like America?" Alex asked.

"It seems very nice, so far," Veronique replied. "Your family is very kind to take me in like this, Alex."

"Oh, I'm sure it'll be fun for us all," Alex answered. "We can all learn about one another."

"Yeah," Ray agreed. "So, where are you from in France?"

"Toulon," Veronique replied. "That's in the southeast. About thirty miles from Marseille."

"It must be lovely there," Alex said with a sigh. "Isn't that a great place for beaches?"

"It is delightful there, *amie*," Veronique answered. "All those boys lounging in the sun . . . It is *très* delightful."

They chatted a while longer. As they finished and cleared off the table, Ray took Alex aside.

"Did you spot it?" he asked her, eyeing Veronique with suspicion.

"Spot what, Ray?" Alex demanded. "Honestly, I don't know what's gotten into you today."

"That French girl made another slip," he insisted. "She said that Toulon is thirty miles from Marseille."

Alex frowned. "So, isn't it?"

"I don't have a clue," Ray admitted. "Geography isn't my strong point. But I do know that they use kilometers in France, not miles. She should have said it was fifty kilometers from Marseille."

"Honestly, Ray!" Alex protested. "You're just getting paranoid. Veronique told us she's trying to improve her English. She's probably also trying to get our system of measurement correct, too."

"Maybe." Ray stared at the newcomer with a scowl. "But I think that there's something wrong with her, and I aim to find out what."

Alex laughed and patted his shoulder. "Ray Alvarado, part-time private eye. Good luck, boy detective." She went to join Veronique.

"Laugh if you like," Ray muttered to himself. "But I'm a regular Sherlock Holmes when I want to be. And I *know* there's something very fishy about that girl—and I aim to find out exactly what."

CHAPTER 5

Alex couldn't figure out why Ray was so antagonistic toward Veronique. The young French girl seemed to be very pleasant, and she was knocking herself out trying to be friendly. Maybe Ray was jealous that Veronique was taking up so much of Alex's time? But that wasn't really very like Ray.

Veronique naturally walked home with Alex. Robyn and Nicole tagged along part of the way, as usual, and they seemed to get along well with Veronique, too. Only Ray, hovering a few paces back, kept aloof from the conversation.

"This seems like a very nice little town," Veronique commented.

"It is," Alex agreed. "We've got a mall just a

short distance from where we live, as well as an amusement park, a bowling alley, a couple of movie theaters, and lots of shops."

Veronique nodded. "And what about factories?" she asked. "Where do people work in this town?"

"Most of them at Paradise Valley Chemical," Robyn replied. "Plenty of the adults work there."

"A chemical plant?" Veronique asked with a shudder. "Isn't that somewhat dangerous?"

"That's what I always wonder," Robyn admitted. "I mean, when you're dealing with all those chemicals it must be toxic city in there."

"It's not bad," Nicole countered. "The plant has a very good safety record. At least recently. They do try to remedy any problems—when they have to."

"No spills or anything?" Veronique asked.

"Well, there was one, a couple of years back," Nicole admitted. "One of their vans crashed and spilled some experimental chemical. But it was cleaned up fast, and there were no problems from it."

"No problems?" Robyn's eyebrows shot up at that. "Excuse me, but what about that kid who got showered in the chemical?"

Nicole sighed. "Honestly, Robyn, that was just

a *rumor*. Let's face it, if anyone took a chemical bath, it would have done all sorts of horrible things to them, wouldn't it? And nobody in our school ever came down with anything. Right, Alex?"

Feeling somewhat hypocritical and embarrassed, Alex was forced to agree with her friend. "I haven't met any one-eyed mutant kids," she said truthfully.

"I don't think it's that simple," Robyn argued, shifting her backpack to her other shoulder. "I'll bet the chemical company found the kid and paid him or her off to keep quiet. Someone might be dying right now, and unable to speak because of the coverup. That sort of thing happens all the time."

"Honestly, Robyn," Nicole said with another sigh. "I'll bet the dictionary has a picture of you in it next to the word *paranoid*." She smiled at Veronique. "Pay no attention to her; she's a professional downer."

"I am not," Robyn objected. "I'm very proud of my amateur status." She shook her head sadly. "Just because I may be paranoid at times doesn't mean I'm wrong about this, you know. I think there really was a chemical kid, and I feel really sorry for whoever it was."

Alex didn't like the way her friend was talking. It made her feel rather scared, in fact. "Oh, come on, Robyn," she argued. "It's been more than two years since the spill. If anyone *had* been seriously injured, we'd know about it by now."

"Alex is right," Nicole agreed. "Anyway, I'm sure this isn't the sort of thing Veronique wants to hear about our lovely town, is it?"

Veronique shrugged. "I am 'ere to learn about everything," she replied. "So I am interested in all you 'ave to say."

"Well, let's talk about something more cheerful," Alex said firmly. "Like, how about going to the mall later? Veronique *has* to see American shops!"

The rest of the walk home was more pleasant, with only Ray glowering at the French girl. Finally even he peeled off to head home, and Alex arrived at her home. Alex gestured to her house.

"Well, here we are," she said modestly. "It's kind of average, I know. But it's home to us."

"It seems lovely," Veronique replied. "Per'aps you could show me around? There is a man who will be bringing my luggage later."

Alex complied. As she was showing Veronique around, the rest of the family arrived home. Her father had collected Mrs. Mack from the local college on the way home, and today had been one of the afternoons when Annie worked at her internship at the plant lab, so she was with them also. Alex introduced Veronique around.

"Enchanté de faire votre connaissance," Annie said to her in perfect French. It made Alex jealous that her sister should be able to do that, while she had problems with even the odd word.

"Please," Veronique said hastily. "It is very sweet of you to try and make me feel at 'ome, but I must practice my English. I would be grateful if you spoke only English to me."

"Oh, sure," Annie agreed. "No problem." She waved a hand. "Got to clean up and help with dinner. Alex, you, too."

"I will also 'elp," Veronique offered.

"Oh, no, that's all right," Mrs. Mack said. "You're our guest, so you just sit back and relax. We'll call you when everything's ready."

Alex set to work in the kitchen and her mother gave her shoulder an affectionate squeeze. "She seems very nice," Mrs. Mack commented. "Are the two of you getting along well?"

"Yes, Mom." Alex smiled. "Everyone at school seems to like her, too. Except for Ray."

"Ray?" Mrs. Mack looked puzzled. "How come he doesn't like her? He's usually the most agreeable person."

"Beats me," Alex confessed. "He just seems to think she's a phony or something."

"If you ask me," Annie offered, "he just resents the fact that she's getting all this attention. You know how he likes to hog the spotlight."

"Well, I'm sure he'll get used to her," Mrs. Mack commented. "Anyway, I thought we'd make chicken cordon bleu for dinner tonight, as a sort of welcoming dish."

Mr. Mack smiled. "A tasty choice," he agreed, obviously relieved they weren't having more vegetarian dishes. "But maybe we should plan some real down-home American meals while she's here? So she gets a taste of our own cooking?"

"I don't think she'd want too much of *our* cooking," Annie muttered to herself.

"I mean like having a barbecue," Mr. Mack explained. "Ribs, steaks, burgers, and so on."

"That would be great for the weekend, George," Mrs. Mack agreed. "I know how you love to play chef over the grill."

"Yay!" Alex agreed. She loved her father's cookouts. There were times when her father was very distracted and sometimes even absent-minded, but when he barbecued, he put all of his considerable energies into it and produced some of the best food she'd ever tasted.

Dinner went well, and afterward the delivery person came with Veronique's trunk and suitcases. After Mrs. Mack had helped the French girl to stow her things away, and made up the fold-out bed, Alex called Nicole and Robyn, and they took Veronique to the mall. As before, Ray hung around with them, a scowl still on his face.

Alex waited until Robyn and Nicole took Veronique into a clothing store, and then she confronted Ray. "Ray, what is your problem with Veronique?" she demanded. "Are you just jealous of the attention she's getting?"

"Me?" Ray seemed to be astonished at the thought. "No way. I just have this gut feeling about her, that's all."

"It's called jealousy," Alex insisted.

"It's called *suspicion*," Ray insisted. "I personally think she's a fake. For example, have you noticed how her accent varies? Sometimes she drops *h*'s from her words and sometimes she doesn't."

"Honestly, Ray," Alex said with a sigh. "Why on Earth would Veronique be anything other than what she seems to be—a perfectly nice, average foreign student?"

"I don't know," Ray admitted. "But I'd bet my saxophone that the girl's a fake. Stick around, and I'll prove it."

"Get over it, Ray," Alex begged. "She's just what she seems to be. Trust me."

"I wish I could," Ray replied. "But I have a bad feeling about that girl. And I know I'm going to be proven right. You wait and see."

Alex sighed. "Okay, Ray. Whatever you say. But keep the crazy suspicions to yourself, please. Don't try and get Nicole and Robyn started."

"All right," Ray agreed. "Anyway, Sherlock Alvarado can solve this case on his own if you refuse to help."

"Whatever you say, Ray," Alex agreed.

Back home again, Alex had to do her music practice. She checked on Veronique first, who was happy to immerse herself in attempting to read the local newspaper to get a taste of American life. Alex headed slowly for her room. Reluctantly, she took the violin out of its case and stared at it. How was she supposed to learn how to play this? It didn't even have any frets! Where were you supposed to put your fingers to play the right notes? Her apprehension growing, she put down the violin and started to study the book that came with it.

After fifteen minutes, she gave up. As near as she could tell, you simply had to *guess* the right place to position your fingers and hope it was right. It would take a genius to play this thing! With a sigh, she tried to hold it in the right position. It was uncomfortable holding the end under her chin, and she had to squint to see if her fingers were in the right places. Then she tried drawing the bow across the strings.

It sounded as if she were murdering several very vocal cats. Even Alex winced at the noise. "Guess the fingering's off," she decided, trying to hold it better. Her next attempt was just as unmusical. Plus, her fingers hurt from pressing on the strings.

This music appreciation was making her appreciate one thing at least—how much skill went into making *real* music. And she had a growing feeling that she simply wasn't going to be able to be one of those people with the skill for doing it.

Annie wandered into the room. "How many people have you murdered in here?" she asked.

"One, counting you," Alex answered. "You think I *like* producing this ghastly noise?"

"Well, I can tell you that nobody in the house is enjoying hearing it," Annie informed her. "Maybe you'd do better to just rethink this whole music business."

"I wish I could," Alex admitted. "But I don't want to just quit. I'd feel like such a failure. Not that *you'd* know much about failing."

Annie gave her a reassuring smile. "I do understand, Alex. And I'm behind you. Even if it does mean hearing more wailing from that thing." She eyed the violin. "Maybe you're just trying too hard."

"That's what you said about my accidents, remember?" Alex reminded her. "Is that your answer to *everything?*"

"With you, pretty much so." Annie sat down on the bed next to her younger sister. "I know how much succeeding means to you. But you don't have to compete constantly to try and get results. If you take it a little easier on yourself, maybe you'd find what you're really good at."

"Maybe." Alex stared at the violin. "I'm beginning to suspect it isn't this, though. Maybe I can switch this for something else tomorrow."

"And don't look at it as a failure," Annie encouraged her. "See it as eliminating an option, but that there are still plenty more to choose from." She grinned. "Just don't try a kettle drum next, okay?"

Alex packed away the violin and went downstairs. Veronique was just finishing some notes on her computer. "How's it going?" Alex asked her.

The French girl closed the file she was working on, then switched off the computer. "It is going well, Alex," she replied. She closed the computer case and slid it down beside the sofa.

Alex frowned slightly. Had she deliberately tried to make sure Alex couldn't see what she was working on? Then Alex lightened up. Ray's suspicions were starting to get to her now. Veronique just didn't like to work with somebody staring over her shoulder, that was all. Alex *hated* to be watched when she did her own work. "You want to watch some TV?"

"Okay," Veronique agreed. "It's *California Beach Patrol* night, isn't it? I love that show!"

Again, Alex's suspicions were aroused. How would a French girl know what day *Beach Patrol* was on? Then she realized that Veronique had probably simply checked out the TV listings in the paper when she had read it. Alex was almost certain she was just letting Ray's suspicions affect her.

Almost certain . . .

CHAPTER 6

For the next two days, things were pretty average. Veronique was quite nice, but having to share a bathroom with another girl as well as Annie didn't help Alex stay on time for things. And the French girl was just full of questions.

Ray was getting more and more convinced that Veronique was definitely faking it. "I asked her some questions today about Paris," he informed Alex, catching up with her as they left history class. "And she told me she'd never been there! Can you imagine it, a French girl who's never been to Paris? Isn't that suspicious?"

"Ray," Alex pointed out, "you're an American and you've never been to Washington, D.C. So what if she's never been to Paris? Is that a crime?"

"It's just very suspicious," Ray insisted. "I think she's up to something. Where is she now?"

"In the library," Alex answered. "I'm going to meet her there."

"I'll come along," Ray said. "I want to ask her a few more questions."

"You're really overdoing this," Alex muttered, but allowed him to accompany her. They found Veronique reading a magazine.

Ray leaned over it. "Reading up on France? Why would you need to do that?"

Veronique closed the magazine. It *had* been an article on France, Alex realized. Veronique frowned. "I was just feeling a little 'ome sick," she confessed. "I mean, I like it 'ere, but . . ." She shrugged.

"A likely story," Ray insisted. "I'm going to get you," he promised Veronique. Glancing at Alex, he added, "See you later." Then he strode out of the library.

Veronique sighed. "Raymond doesn't like me, does he?" she asked, picking up her bag.

Alex helped Veronique load her bag and then they left the library together. "It's not that Ray doesn't like you," Alex argued. "It's just that he's got this idea that you're a fake from somewhere, and he's desperate to prove himself correct. He's likely to be like this for a few more days yet. Then he'll realize he was wrong and settle down."

"I 'ope so," Veronique said. "I feel like I am being interrogated constantly by 'im." She shrugged and smiled. "Then again, since I ask so many questions myself, I should not complain when 'e asks me some, should I?"

Alex laughed at the thought. But she noticed that there seemed to be some concern in Veronique's eyes. Ray must really be starting to bug the foreign girl. Maybe she'd better have words with him. It wasn't fair that he should be picking on a girl who was probably suffering from homesickness.

Later that day, Alex went over to Nicole's house to see Robyn and Nicole. She'd hardly had the time for a couple of days, since she'd been shepherding Veronique about.

"Free of your charge at last?" Robyn asked sympathetically.

"Yeah." Alex stretched out on the bed. "She went to meet Mom at the college and get a tour. So I get a break." She sighed. "I like her and everything, but it's starting to feel like I've got another sister. And I *definitely* feel that one sister is more than enough."

"I agree," Nicole said. "And she asks such

weird questions, too. You know what she asked me today? If I knew of anyone in school who might have lost a lot of weight in the past couple of years!"

"She asked you that?" Alex was puzzled. "Maybe she's trying to find out about fad diets, or something."

Robyn snorted. "She asked me if anyone had suddenly changed their hair color in the past couple of years." She held up a strand of her own russet locks. "Like I would *want* to change to this lovely color?"

Alex didn't get it. "Maybe she's just surveying fashion trends, or something?"

"Maybe," Nicole said doubtfully. She tossed a pillow to Robyn, who settled down on the floor with it. "I just think she's a little weird at times, that's all. Did you see her in gym class today? When we had to do the rope climbing?"

"I hate that," Robyn said, with a wince. "I'm sure it gives me blisters."

"Yeah," Nicole pointed out, "but Veronique shimmied right up the ropes like she was born to it. Under that air of French sophistication, she's quite an athlete."

Alex frowned. "Your point being?"

"I'm not sure," Nicole admitted. "It's just that I didn't expect it from her, that's all. I guess I'm prejudiced or something, but I expected a French girl to be more laid back. She's starting to remind me of a census taker."

"Yeah," Robyn agreed, cross-legged on the pillow, looking as if she were about to start meditating. "Or one of those poll people in the mall that's always interfering with your shopping and asking you dumb questions about which brand of cola you prefer. I always hate that."

"Right," Nicole agreed. "As if I drink *cola!* It's an invasion of our privacy to ask us things like that."

"Exactly," Robyn said. "Only our parents and our teachers have the right to ask us questions. What do you think, Alex?"

Alex grinned. "I think that was a question, and you don't have any right to ask me it!" The three of them broke up laughing. But what her friends had said stuck in Alex's mind. Veronique's questions did seem to be a little odd at times. Maybe it was just her way . . . or, just maybe, Ray might have something after all. What if he was correct, and she wasn't what she seemed to be?

Then what?

At dinner that night, Veronique turned her attention on Alex's father. "You must 'ave a very important job," she told him at one point.

"Well," Mr. Mack answered modestly, "I don't know that I'd really call it *important*." He frowned, concentrating. "On the other hand, yes, I suppose it is, really. I do a lot of the research into the effects of the various chemicals that our company produces, so that we'll be absolutely certain that they're safe once they're released for the general public to buy."

"It is a very responsible job," Veronique replied. "It must be very . . . 'ow do you say it? Challenging and fulfilling?"

"Well, yes, I do get a great deal of satisfaction out of it," Mr. Mack confessed. "It's very intriguing tracking all the potential effects even the smallest chemicals can have on people. . . . It's also sometimes very tedious, I'm afraid. That's why it often takes so long for some chemicals to be released after they've been developed."

"That must be very frustrating for your bosses," Veronique suggested. "Do they ever try to . . . 'urry things along, if you see what I mean?"

Mr. Mack was a little bothered. "Well, obviously they would like me to get the results as quickly as possible," he agreed. "But they would never want me to speed things up at the expense of thorough, careful testing."

Veronique nodded. "Like with this . . . what is it? GC-161?"

Alex tried hard not to choke on her lasagna and managed to turn it into a coughing fit instead. Where had Veronique learned the name of the chemical? She covered her confusion by taking a large sip of lemonade.

"You know about that?" Mr. Mack asked, amazed. "I didn't think it was already known in France." He looked rather alarmed. "There must have been a major security leak, which we'll have to look into."

"No," Veronique said hastily. "It is not known at all in France, as far as I know. It is just that I heard at school that there had been an accident involving it and some poor child."

"Oh, that old story." Mr. Mack shrugged, scraping a few more string beans onto his plate. "There's no evidence of any truth to that rumor," he assured her. "And if someone *had* been doused in GC-161, I'm sure we'd have all heard about it by now. After all, I'm certain that it would have some *very* strange effects on a human body."

That intrigued Veronique. She put down her fork and prompted: "Such as?"

Annie caught the warning look Alex flashed her. "Dad," she said hastily, "this is supposed to be secret research, remember. I mean, I'm sure Veronique doesn't mean to pry, and would never want to pass along the information, but . . ."

"Oh, right," her father agreed. "Loose lips sink ships, eh?" He smiled apologetically at Veronique. "I'm sorry, but Annie's quite correct. I really am not allowed to talk about my work."

"I understand," Veronique replied. Alex wasn't certain, but the French girl looked rather annoyed at her request being turned down. "I would not wish to cause you problems over something that is no more than mild curiosity on my part."

"No problem," Mr. Mack said. He reached for the dish in the center of the table. "Anyone for more vegetarian lasagna? This is rather good, isn't it?"

After dinner, Annie dragged Alex aside. She was frowning and watching Veronique, who was making some notes on her computer in the living room. "Alex," she said softly and urgently. "What was all that about? How come she knows the name of GC-161? I'm sure that's not general knowledge."

"It isn't," Alex agreed. "She *has* been asking questions about the accident, though. But nobody at school knows the name of the chemical involved. So how does she know it?"

"Right." Annie's eyes narrowed suspiciously. "And she was trying to get information out of Dad on what effects the stuff could have on a human being."

Alex didn't like the sound of where this conversation was going. "You think she's looking for *me?*" she asked. Then she remembered what Robyn and Nicole had mentioned. "Come to think of it, she's been asking odd questions. Like if anyone lost a lot of weight, or suddenly changed their hair color." She swallowed. "And Ray's been saying for days that he thinks she's some kind of fake."

"Ray can be pretty perceptive at times," Annie said. "And this may be one of those times. It's just suspicions so far, but I think we'd do well to be very careful around Veronique for the time being. And watch out for anything that might prove Ray's theories."

Alex nodded reluctantly. "Maybe I misjudged him," she admitted. "It looks like he could be right, after all."

"Okay. Let's just play it nice and cool," Annie decided. "Until we get some proof, we really can't be sure of anything. Just keep your eyes and ears peeled for now, okay?"

"Okay," Alex agreed. She glanced at the French girl with some concern. "I just hope we're wrong, and this is just some silly thing she's got into her mind."

"So do I," Annie agreed. "But we have to take precautions. I don't want to see anyone experimenting on my kid sister except me."

A little while later, Veronique managed to make an excuse and get out of the Mack house on her own. It was harder than she'd expected to keep up her disguise every single day. But she knew she was doing fine, and she was rather proud of herself. Still, it was time to check in with Uncle Vince. He'd set up a series of contacts for her before they had begun this mission, and she knew exactly where he'd be right now.

Two blocks from the Mack house was a telephone truck, parked near a switching box. There was no sign of anyone working, though. Veronique rapped on the back door of the truck: two short, one long.

The door popped open. Vince, dressed as a telephone repairman, glared out. "Get in," he commanded, scanning the street to be certain she hadn't been followed. Then he closed the door behind her again. "Well," he growled, "how's it going?"

Veronique pulled off her long blond wig. "Whew! I'm glad to be out of that." She scratched at the stubble on her head. "It's horribly hot in there. And I'm getting sick of being asked for fashion tips at that dumb school. Those kids think I really *like* these goofy outfits." She pawed her lacy blouse with distaste.

"Spare me the fashion report," Vince complained. "Tell me about your mission. How are you doing?"

"Pretty good," Veronique told him. "The Mack family have accepted me without problems, and the kids at school seem to like me—on the whole. They're answering most of my questions, and I'm following up on a couple of leads."

"*On the whole?*" Vince repeated. "What's that supposed to mean?"

"Well, there's one kid, Raymond Alvarado, who thinks I'm a fake," Veronique admitted.

"What?" Vince almost exploded. "He's onto you?"

"No, I don't think so," Veronique hastily assured him. "He's just one of those pain-in-the-neck types who doesn't seem to like me for some reason. He says he'll prove I'm a fake, but he's having no luck so far."

Vince scowled. "You must have done something to make him suspicious."

"I don't think so," Veronique answered. "Anyway, none of the other kids believe him at all. They think he's just trying to get attention. So, he can't have any real reason to doubt me. Maybe he's just jealous. I'm pretty popular with the other kids. A lot of them like to hang out with the *new girl*. It must be my terrific French accent that does it." Then she scowled. "Hey, you don't suppose that GC-161 can make people able to read your thoughts, do you? Maybe he's the kid, and can read my mind?"

"I don't know *what* GC-161 can do," Vince answered unhappily. "Neither does anyone else I've spoken to. What about the Macks' father? Did you get anything out of him yet?"

"No," Veronique admitted. "I did try, but his daughter, Annie, made him switch the subject. She seems to be awfully quick. If I can talk to him without her around, then maybe I can get more information out of him. Trust me, Uncle Vince, I'll nail this kid and get you all the information you'll ever want on GC-161."

"Good." Vince scowled as he thought. "Look, I'm going to put feelers out to Ms. Atron and see if she'll talk to me about our plan. If I can just get back into her good books again . . . this might well do it." He smiled down at his niece. "Okay, Vincie, get back to work. Let's see if we can grab this kid sometime in the next week or so. If we do, I promise you that you'll be able to chose anything you want to do from here on in. If Ms. Atron has reason to be grateful to you, there's nothing she wouldn't do for you."

"I like the sound of that," Veronique admitted, replacing her wig. "And I promise you fast results, Uncle Vince."

"Good." Vince smiled again, nastily. "We'll get the kid and then get the rewards. Trust me, Vincie, if you do this right, then this is just the start of a long and beautiful partnership. Now, back to work!"

Veronique hopped out of the van and made her way back to the Mack house.

From behind a bush down the road, Ray peered out and watched her leave. He'd caught a glimpse of the occupant of the van, and it was a face he knew very well. "Vince," he whispered to himself. "So he's behind all this. Alex is going to *have* to listen to me now."

CHAPTER 7

Alex had been putting off practicing the tuba most of the evening, but she knew she couldn't get out of it much longer. Veronique had gone to take one of her long soaks in the tub, so she didn't have the French girl to worry about in case anything happened. With a sigh, she hauled out the case and opened it.

Annie glanced up from the work she was doing at her desk. "Am I likely to regret staying in the room with you and that thing?" she asked.

"Probably," Alex agreed glumly. "So far, I've not exactly been having much luck with this music-appreciation stuff." She stared at the tuba as if it were a snake about to strike. "I doubt this will be much different." She opened the instruction book and tried to hold the tuba correctly, positioning her fingers. "Here goes."

Alex blew a long, mournful low note. It was actually surprisingly musical, and for a split second, she thought that maybe she'd found her instrument at last. Then her whole body tingled, and with a rush of panic, she felt herself morphing into a puddle of liquid again.

"Alex?"

In utter panic now, Alex heard her father's voice from her parents' bedroom, then his footsteps. He was coming to see what was wrong! And if he caught her in this state . . . she didn't know whether to try and flow somewhere to hide or to try morphing back into her real form. Did she have time for the latter? But she *couldn't* hide! He knew she was in here, practicing.

Annie came to the rescue again, blocking the door from opening, as their father tapped on it. "Alex?" he called again. "Is everything all right?"

Concentrating hard, and trying to stifle the panic welling inside of her, Alex began to reform.

"Everything's fine, Dad," Annie called hastily. "She just dropped the tuba on her toe. You know how awkward that thing can be sometimes."

"Oh." Mr. Mack sounded almost satisfied.

Then he added, "Annie, would you mind terribly if I had a private word with Alex?"

Alex was finally re-formed, but still shaking slightly from her ordeal. She glanced at Annie and nodded.

"Sure thing, Dad," Annie replied, opening the door with a cheery smile. "You two probably need some quality time together anyhow. I'll leave you to it."

Alex picked up the tuba rather dispiritedly and placed it on the bed. "Sorry about the noise," she apologized. "I guess I didn't have as good a grip on it as I thought I had."

"That's okay, Alex," her father replied, putting an arm about her shoulder. "These things happen." He smiled encouragingly at her. "Alex, you seem to be really keen on this music urge of yours. But perhaps you've picked the wrong instrument? It reminds me of my youth, you know." He smiled at a memory. "I really wanted to play the saxophone, like Ray can. And I was terrible at it. Then *my* father came up with a solution." He was struck by a sudden idea. "In fact, it's one that might well work for you. I think I still have it somewhere . . ." He thought for a moment and then snapped back to reality. "I just have to look for it." He gave Alex's shoulder a reassuring squeeze. "I think I may have the answer for you by tomorrow, Alex. So don't give up yet. Give your old father a chance to help, okay?"

"You bet," Alex promised. She had no idea what he had in mind, but he was trying to help her, and that was what counted.

"Good." Her father went to the door of the room. Then he looked back. "Meanwhile, maybe you'd better give that tuba a rest," he suggested.

"I *definitely* agree with that!" Alex slipped it back into its case and locked it firmly. Tomorrow, she'd return it to Miss Henderson, with apologies.

Annie returned a few minutes later. "So, what was that all about?" she asked, settling back to her work.

"I'm not sure," Alex admitted. "Dad seems to think he can help me with this music thing, but I don't know. I guess I'm just not cut out for the life of a musician."

"Well, you'd better forget that multimillion-dollar pop recording contract then," Annie answered with a grin. "And we do know that your involuntary morphing can be induced by low notes played on the tuba as well as the trombone. I'm more certain than ever that it must be harmonic oscillation that causes it."

"Whatever," Alex agreed, not certain what

Annie even meant. "It does mean I'm steering clear of big, heavy wind instruments in the future, though."

"Smart decision." Annie made notes in her journal about Alex's condition. "And, speaking of which, we have to make up our minds about Veronique."

"Yeah." That was another problem that Alex couldn't just hope would go away. "If she is a spy, what is she after? Me, or GC-161?"

"It could be either," Annie decided. "Or both. Or we could just both be overly suspicious, and she may be simply what she appears to be."

"Yeah." Alex sat on her bed, cross-legged. "Well, we have to find out, one way or another."

At that moment, the bathroom door opened, and Veronique walked out. "Allo," she greeted them through the open bedroom door. "I am sorry to 'ave taken so long, but I adore a lengthy soak."

"No problem," Annie replied. "Glad you're enjoying your stay."

Veronique nodded. "Very much so," she said. "Well, I 'ave to go and make some more notes. I 'ave a long report to prepare when I am finished 'ere."

"I bet she does," Annie muttered to herself as

72

the other girl hurried down the stairs. "Alex, did you notice something odd about her?"

Alex frowned. "No. Like what?"

"Like," Annie explained, leaning forward and keeping her voice low, "the fact that she was in the bathroom for half an hour, taking a long soak. Yet her hair is bone dry."

Alex considered the point. "Maybe she used a bathcap?" she suggested. "Or a hair dryer?"

"I didn't hear a dryer," Annie said firmly. "And no bath cap is *that* water-tight. You always get some of your hair wet when you take a bath."

"Yeah," Alex replied thoughtfully. "Do you really think she *didn't* have a bath, then?"

"I don't know," Annie admitted. "But I do know that there's something very odd about Veronique. And I'm afraid that it may well have something to do with you."

Alex scowled, worried. "You think she suspects that I'm the GC-161 kid, and that's why she's in the house?"

"Maybe." Annie put her hand over Alex's. "Just don't start panicking, or anything yet. Let's see if we can get some proof that she *is* a spy first. Then we'll have to find out what it is she's after."

Uneasily, Alex nodded. She didn't like the

thought that Veronique might be hot on her trail. Was she finally going to be exposed and then taken off? She'd met Danielle Atron several times in the past, and she knew that there was very little that Ms. Atron wouldn't do to get whatever it was she wanted. And she had a tough security force, who could keep a lot of things hidden. If Ms. Atron ever had Alex fall into her clutches, Alex knew that there wasn't much chance of being saved from her experiments.

The very thought of that was enough to make Alex shiver.

Whatever happened, she couldn't allow herself to be exposed!

She was still worrying later, when she went to fix herself a snack. As she was pouring a glass of juice, the phone rang. "Got it!" she yelled first, snatching up the receiver. "Hi, Mack residence."

"Alex!" It was Ray, his voice sounding very worried. "We've got trouble—serious trouble. Meet me in front of your house right away. We have to talk where we can't be overheard. And don't tell me I'm just being overdramatic, because I'm not."

"Okay." Alex hung up, forgetting about the snack. She hurried through the living room, where her mother was working on some papers. Veronique was in the corner, tapping notes into her computer. At least she'd be out of the way for a while. "Uh, I've just got to go out a few minutes," Alex told her mother. "Ray wants to check some homework out with me. I'll be quick, I promise."

"Okay," her mother agreed absently.

Alex hurried out and down to the end of their driveway. Ray hurried up to meet her, glancing all around as he did so.

"Alex," he asked anxiously, "do you know where Veronique is?"

"Sure," she replied. "In our living room, updating her computer files. Ray, I'm sorry I didn't believe you about her before, but it seemed like such a silly idea—"

"Whoa!" he exclaimed, surprised. "You mean you *do* believe me now?"

"Yeah." Alex explained what had happened at dinner. "It certainly looks like she's a spy," she finished. "You were right all along."

"It's worse than that," Ray told her. "When she left your house earlier this evening, I followed her. She met up with Vince."

"Vince!" The creepy security man always gave Alex the shivers. Ms. Atron might be cold and unfeeling, but Vince actually enjoyed his job.

What Ms. Atron would do as a duty, Vince would do for pleasure. "You're sure?"

"Saw him with my own eyes—large as life, and twice as ugly." Ray lost his smirk then. "Alex, do you think that Veronique was planted in your house because they suspect you of being the GC-161 kid, or is it just coincidence?"

"I *hope* it's coincidence," Alex replied, even more worried than he was. "But I don't think it would be very safe to assume that."

"Me, neither," Ray agreed. "So, what do we do now?"

"I'm going to have to talk this over with Annie," Alex decided. "She's got more brains than even she knows what to do with. I really need her advice. But it seems to me that we've got to find out what Veronique is after." She tapped her chin thoughtfully, as she glanced back at her home. It had always seemed so safe, a haven to rest in—until now. At this moment, her biggest problem ever was waiting in there for her to return. As she thought about it, she could see Veronique talking with her mother in the living room. *Pumping her for more information?* Alex wondered.

"And I'll bet the answers are all in that computer she carries with her," Ray said. "Okay, let's try not to panic. You talk to Annie, and maybe we can come up with some sort of plan. I'll talk to you again tomorrow."

"Right."

Ray put a friendly hand on her arm. "Alex, be careful. You've got a snake sharing the house with you right now."

"Don't I know it." She managed a watery smile. "Thanks, Ray. You're a better friend than I deserve. Thanks for sticking to your convictions even when I didn't believe you."

"You're just as good a friend to me, Alex," Ray replied. "So take care. I don't want to have to break in a new best friend."

Alex nodded and hurried back into the house.

Her mother glanced up from the sofa, where she and Veronique had been chatting. "Everything okay, Alex?" she asked.

"Sure," Alex answered, glancing at Veronique. "Everything's fine. No problems." She only wished that it was true. As Ray had said, she was sharing her house with a snake—one that might strike at any moment. . . .

CHAPTER 8

It was difficult for Alex to act as if nothing had happened to change things, but somehow she managed. If Veronique noticed that Alex was a little jittery around her, she didn't say anything. Obviously the French girl—or whatever and whoever she was—didn't realize that Alex was suspicious of her. As they headed for school the following morning, she was chattering away about the upcoming school basketball playoffs and spring break. Alex just nodded and muttered agreement from time to time, which seemed to keep Veronique happy.

Ray joined them, looking fairly serious for Ray. "How's the music world?"

Alex sighed. "Dad says he's got the answer to

my problem, but he wouldn't tell me what it was. He likes to cultivate the air of mystery."

"Fathers are like that," Veronique offered.

"Oh?" Alex asked, with interest. "Is *yours* like that?"

Veronique paused, obviously thinking hard. Alex had a feeling that the other girl was going to lie, for some reason. She just had that "how do I get out of this?" look on her face. "Not really," she finally answered. "My father is a very strong man. He 'as a will of steel, and over-comes all obstacles. He is a real man."

Ray sniffed loudly. "It's a shame he doesn't have a *real* daughter, then," he commented.

Suddenly Veronique lost her composure, as if this latest insult had struck home where none of Ray's previous comments had. She whirled around and grabbed a fistful of his T-shirt, hauling him in close. "What do you mean by that?" she hissed angrily.

Not at all worried, Ray gave her a cheerful smile. "Your accent's slipping," he said.

Veronique obviously struggled to calm down. She released his shirt and stepped back. "I am sorry," she apologized. "Per'aps they are right when they say watching television makes you violent. I 'ave been watching too many American crime shows, I think."

79

Ray raised an eyebrow, obviously not buying the explanation for a second. Neither did Alex.

"Sometimes things boil over," she said, hoping that Veronique thought she was still fooled. Thankfully, at this moment Nicole and Robyn joined them, then started chattering away. Ray managed to drag Alex back a short distance.

"So," he said quietly, "that shows her true colors, don't you think? Well, did the family genius come up with anything approaching a plan?"

"Not really," Alex admitted glumly.

"Hey, then leave it to Sherlock Alvarado," Ray said confidently. "I'll come up with a plan. They don't call me 'Sneaky' for nothing."

"They don't call you 'Sneaky' at all," Alex objected.

"Well, after this they will," Ray vowed. "You wait and see."

Alex couldn't help but smile at his confidence. "Okay," she said.

At least school distracted Alex from her problems for a while. She returned the tuba to Miss Henderson, relieved not to have to carry the weight around. "I'm not dropping out of musical appreciation, really," Alex explained. "My father thinks he's got a solution, but he hasn't told me what it is yet."

"All right, Alex," Miss Henderson agreed. "I really hope that you do find something that you like. As I said, the aim of this program is to make you like music more, not less."

The rest of the day went by pretty much as normal. At lunchtime, Nicole joined Alex. "That Veronique is starting to wear down my patience," Nicole announced, sliding into the chair next to Alex and opening her brown bag.

Seeing the French girl seated apart, making notes, Alex didn't mind discussing her. "What did she do now?"

Nicole sighed. "She's asking everyone if they know of anyone whose grades changed suddenly in the past two years, either up or down dramatically. What is *with* her? She doesn't even know her French geography very well. And they say *American* kids are badly taught?"

Alex didn't know whether to confide her suspicions about Veronique to Nicole or not. She didn't want to leave her friend out, but she knew that there might be complications if she told Nicole. Nicole was one of those people who confronted problems head-on, refusing to back down until they were solved. This made her a terrific student and a great friend, but it could complicate matters if she confronted Veronique. What if the so-called French girl really was some kind of spy trying to expose Alex? In that case, confronting her directly might lead her to accusing Alex in public. That would be an utter disaster.

"Maybe she's just not a very good student?" she finally suggested.

"Then why would she get selected to participate in a student exchange program?" Nicole asked reasonably. "You have to *earn* your place in this scheme." She scowled. "You know, I'm starting to think that there's something not quite right about the girl."

Uh-oh! Nicole was starting to get on the trail of the truth now. Alex chewed nervously at her lip, wondering what the best thing to do was. "That's what Ray thinks," she finally admitted. "But you know how paranoid he can get sometimes." She crushed her empty milk carton and pitched it into the nearest garbage can. For once, she made a perfect shot—not even any rim.

"Yes," Nicole agreed, cautiously. "But maybe this time he's right."

"Well, let's leave the investigation to him for now," Alex suggested. "If he can't handle it, then maybe we should lend a hand. We don't want to butt in where we're not wanted."

It was a pretty weak argument, and Nicole looked less than happy with it. "I guess," she finally said. "But if he doesn't have some answers by Monday, I'm going to ask Veronique some very pointed questions."

Ouch! Just what Alex didn't need—a time limit on her problem. She *had* to sort out Veronique before Nicole—and, most likely, Robyn, too— started to poke around.

Thankfully, on her way home that afternoon, she was struck with an idea. When she, Veronique, and Ray reached home, Annie was already there. Veronique excused herself to make more of her endless notes, which saved Alex the trouble of having to think of some excuse to get rid of her. The three of them headed for Alex and Annie's room.

"We've *got* to take a look at that computer of hers," Alex said firmly. "Nicole and Robyn are starting to get suspicious of her now, and if they look around, they might find out things about me."

"Right," Ray agreed. "But *how?* She never lets that thing out of her sight."

"Yes, she does," Alex said eagerly. "She's in the habit of taking half-hour long baths every night. I'm sure she'll do that tonight. We can get her computer then." Alex glanced at her sister. "Do you think you can break into her files in a half-hour?"

Annie frowned in concentration. "Maybe. But I'd prefer having an hour. I'm good, but sometimes these things can be a real problem."

"Okay," Alex said. "Look, I'll figure out some way to keep Veronique upstairs for an hour. You and Ray use the time to go over her laptop."

"Then what?" Ray asked.

"Whatever we do next depends on what information we can find out from Veronique," Annie said. "We have to know what she's up to, and how much she knows or has guessed."

Ray nodded. "This sounds like fun. No more Sherlock Alvarado—now it's Agent Double-oh-eight . . ." He held his hand like a gun. "Secret agent man."

Alex rolled her eyes. "This is no time for games, Ray. It's serious!"

"Hey," Ray objected. "I know it's serious. But that doesn't mean we can't have some fun doing it, does it?"

"Okay," Annie agreed, to stop the argument. "Now, she takes her bath at eight. Ray, can you be back here then?"

"You bet." He grinned. "Should we synchronize watches, or something?"

"I don't think that'll be necessary," Annie replied. "Just don't be late."

84

"You got it." With a cheery grin and a wave, Ray left.

Finally, Alex thought, *we're doing something*. And later that evening, they would get some answers from Veronique. . . .

After dinner, Alex's father took her aside. "I found what I was looking for," he told her happily. "The answer to your problem." He took a small package from his desk and handed it to her. "It's my old tin whistle."

Alex removed the whistle from its pouch. There was a small instructions book with it, far less intimidating than the ones she'd been studying for the other instruments. "You play the whistle?" she asked, amazed.

"Well, not for a long time," Mr. Mack admitted. "It's sort of a family thing. As you know, my family was originally from Europe, and these little whistles are pretty traditional over there. This one belonged to my grandfather, and he taught me to play it when I was about your age. It's pretty simple to learn, and I'll bet you can pick it up in no time."

Alex studied the whistle with interest. It was about eight inches long, with six holes in the top and one underneath. It looked like a child's toy flute. It was certainly the lightest instrument she'd tried yet! "So, how come you didn't give this to Annie?" she asked.

Mr. Mack shrugged. "Annie's not really into music," he explained. "But since you seemed to be so keen on learning to play something, I thought it would be perfect for you. Now, let me just show you how to hold it and play it." He demonstrated, covering some of the holes in the top of the whistle with his fingers. Then he blew a beautiful clear note. "You change notes by covering up different combinations of holes," he explained. "Now, you have a try."

Taking the whistle gingerly, Alex was glad that it produced high notes, and not the low ones that seemed to be making her morph. She tried to hold it the way her father had. He adjusted her grip slightly, moving her little finger to fully cover a hole, then nodded to her. Placing the whistle to her lips, Alex blew.

And a crisp clear note emerged.

Excitedly, Alex tried a different finger combination, producing a second note.

"This is easy," she exclaimed happily. "You know, Dad, I really think I might be able to get the hang of this."

"That's the spirit," her father encouraged. "I think you're right. All it will take is a little practice, and we'll have you playing it like a professional in no time."

Throwing her arms around him, Alex gave him a big hug. "You're a genius, Dad. You know that? Thank you so much."

"I'm just glad that I could help," he replied honestly. "I know that there are a lot of problems you have that only Annie or your mother can help you with. It makes me happy when there's one I can offer advice on." He patted her affectionately on the head.

"I don't know what I'd do without you," Alex told him. Snatching up the pouch and book, she grinned. "I'm going to do an hour's practice right now," she promised. "I'm going to make you proud of me."

Mr. Mack beamed. "Alex, I'm *always* proud of you," he said. "But I don't mind being even more proud of you."

Dashing upstairs, Alex felt quite excited. This whistle was a lot easier for her to play, and it seemed to produce only high-pitched notes, so there was no danger of her morphing while she played it. Plus, it was quite easy to learn. She really felt she had a chance now to get the extra credit for musical appreciation! That would be absolutely marvelous.

The practice went well, and by the end of the

hour, she was playing "Frère Jacques," at a reasonable speed, as well as "Saint Patrick's Day" obviously a bit slowly. But she didn't care. She was making music, and she knew she'd be able to speed up her fingering with just a little practice every day. And that wouldn't be such a hardship.

Annie knocked and entered their room. "Dad came through, eh?"

"Yes," Alex agreed, grinning widely. "And I really think I'm getting the hang of this. It's fun."

"Good." Annie smiled at her kid sister. "I'm pleased. Now, it's almost eight, so we'd better get ready. Veronique is just packing her notes away, so she's going to be hitting the bathtub any moment now. You'd better get ready for whatever it is you aim to do."

Alex slid the whistle into its pouch and put it away. "I figured that once she's settled in, I'd morph into the bathroom and hide her clothes," she explained. "That way, she'll be stuck until she finds them again. Or calls for help. And if she happens to see me, she'll just think she's splashed on the floor, or something."

"It could work," Annie agreed. "But you don't need to take all of her clothes. Just her T-shirt, maybe."

"Okay." Alex could grab it quite simply by reforming briefly, then taking the clothes with her when she morphs again. The shower curtain would shield her from Veronique for the quick second she needed.

The two of them ambled out of their room and toward the stairs. Veronique was heading up, looking cheery. "Allo," she greeted them. "I am just about to 'ave my bath."

"Lovely," Annie replied.

"Enjoy a good long soak," Alex replied, trying hard not to giggle. She was going to make absolutely certain that it was longer than Veronique expected.

CHAPTER 9

Veronique went into the bathroom. Partway down the stairs, Alex and Annie halted. They could see both of their parents in the kitchen, talking.

"They're occupied," Annie said gratefully. "You go and make certain that Veronique stays put. I'll grab her laptop, let Ray in, and then meet you in our bedroom. Okay?"

"No problem," Alex answered quietly. She tiptoed back upstairs and stood outside the bathroom door, listening. She could hear the sound of running water, which meant that Veronique was still running her bath. Another few minutes, then, before she was in it. Then give her a couple of minutes to start relaxing, so she wouldn't spot Alex coming under the door. . . .

Alex paced about, impatiently. She had nothing to do for the moment but wait, and she hated that. Finally the five minutes she had allowed Veronique to relax were over. Glancing down the stairs to make certain her parents wouldn't interrupt her and see something they shouldn't, Alex then morphed into her liquid state. As always, everything seemed so weird in this state. She could see while she was like this and hear what was going on around her.

Quickly and almost soundlessly, Alex squished her body and slid under the bathroom door. Just inside, she paused, checking that it was safe to go ahead.

Veronique was obviously enjoying herself. The bathtub was almost full, and there were mounds of bubbles. The other girl was totally relaxed, her head back and resting on the end of the tub, her eyes closed tightly under a blue gel mask.

And . . . Alex couldn't look surprised in this state, but she could feel it.

Veronique didn't have the long hair that she should have had!

Alex didn't get it at first. Then she saw the long blond wig hanging over the back of the chair where Veronique's clothing lay, and she understood. It was a disguise! But why did she need one?

Concentrating hard to get as clear a picture as she could, Alex finally clicked. The close-cropped hair that Veronique really had was the final clue. Even more worried than she had been before, Alex realized that she was looking at a younger female version of Vince.

She had to be some relative of his. Alex couldn't imagine Vince even marrying and having children, so she must be a niece or maybe even a younger sister.

This changed Alex's plans slightly. Instead of stealing an item of Veronique's clothing, Alex slipped quietly over to the chair, morphed silently back to her human form, and picked up the wig. Then she melted down to liquid again, taking the wig with her. Alex was watching Veronique constantly, to see if the other girl had noticed anything, but she was safe. Veronique was still lying back, her eyes closed, blissfully unaware of what was happening just a couple of feet away from her.

Alex just hoped she stayed that way until she'd made her escape.

Once she'd absorbed the wig, Alex slithered back slowly to the bathroom door. She wanted to get out fast, but she was afraid that Veronique might see a flash of light reflecting from her or hear the sound of her movement. She didn't have lungs as such in her liquid state, or she'd have breathed a sigh of relief once she'd passed under the door and out into the corridor again. She checked that her parents weren't in sight, then morphed back into her human form, holding the blond wig in her right hand.

"Gotcha!" she murmured softly to herself, grinning smugly at the bathroom door. Then she hurried to her room.

Annie and Ray were there, and Ray looked up as she entered.

"Hi, Alex," he said, his eyes widening. "What's that?"

"Our guarantee that Veronique won't budge from the bathroom until we want her to," Alex replied cheerfully. "It's the reason her hair never gets wet when she takes a bath. This is the wig she uses."

Annie stared at it in surprise. "A wig? Whatever for?"

"Because she has short-cut hair," Alex explained. "She looks a lot like Vince. I think she's related to him somehow." She hoisted the wig like a trophy. "Anyway, she won't dare leave the bathroom without this. I'll just keep it until you're done, then slip it back in again."

"Good work, Alex," Annie said approvingly. She gestured to her desk, where she had Veronique's laptop hooked into her own computer. "I was just getting started. As I guessed, the files are all encrypted. You need a password to access them."

"Think you'll be able to do it?" Alex asked anxiously.

"Sure," Annie replied with confidence. "Child's play."

Alex grinned. "Go get 'em."

Annie concentrated for the next ten minutes, muttering under her breath as she ran a diagnostic probe to try and access the laptop's files. Again and again, the words *Access Denied* came up on the screen. Alex was just starting to worry that, despite her confidence, Annie might not be able to do this when, suddenly, the screen changed.

"Bingo!" Annie murmured happily. "I've broken the codes."

"Way to go!" Ray said enthusiastically, pushing forward for a better look at what was coming up on Annie's computer screen. "Wow, there's a lot of stuff in there."

"I told you she makes a lot of notes," Alex commented. "Annie, what's the most important file there?"

"Hard to say," Annie answered. "I'm copying them all to a disc, so we can study them later if we like. Right now, there are a couple I'd like to check out, though, as soon as the copying's finished."

Alex bit her lip and twined strands of hair nervously through her fingers while they waited. They were so close now to discovering what was going on. It was so frustrating to have to wait even a few more minutes.

"Okay, that's done," Annie finally announced. She scrolled down the menu and highlighted a file named *GC-161*. "This should be important," she said, opening the file.

Alex and Ray both leaned forward for a good look at what came up on the screen. It was a report about the accident, followed by notes, obviously made by Vince, about his unsuccessful search for the victim. Then came a bunch of scientific notes, which lost Alex almost immediately. "What does all that say?" she asked plaintively.

"Basically, it's a summary of what Vince had managed to gather about GC-161 before Danielle fired him," Annie answered. "It's pretty good, but, of course, Dad's come up with some new material since then that Vince couldn't have known about. Veronique was apparently asking Dad about some of this, because the last couple of notes are definitely written by an amateur."

"But what about searching for *me?*" Alex asked.

"Isn't that the most important thing? We have to *know* what she knows—or even suspects."

"Okay," Annie agreed, closing the file. "Let's see . . . it looks like she's got a file on just about every kid in school, so yours should be . . . here." She stopped the cursor on the line marked *Mack, Alexandra* and then clicked onto it.

The file opened up, and Alex leaned forward, eager and anxious to discover what it said.

The first page was just general stuff about her—birth date, weight, height, and school grades, some of which made Alex wince. Then came the good stuff. There was a heading for *GC-161?* and then a short report:

Chances that this subject is the sought-after accident victim are almost zero. Alex (as she prefers to be called) is a thoroughly average kid, with absolutely no outstanding features except one of the most boring lives I've ever known. No outstanding characteristics, no known possible disabilities. I'd scratch her from consideration....

Alex's cheeks were burning with indignation. *"Boring life?"* she exclaimed. "What a horrible, untrue thing to say!"

"Hey, Alex," Ray replied, grinning heavily, "look on the bright side. She's absolutely convinced that you're *not* the kid she's after. You're free and clear."

"Yes," Alex agreed, still hurt. "But did she have to be so nasty about me?"

"It's excellent camouflage," Annie pointed out. "When Vince sees this, he's *definitely* going to leave you alone. In fact," she added with a smile, "after reading that, *I'm* tempted to leave your boring life alone." Then, when she saw Alex's face fall, she said hastily, "I'm sorry, Alex. I shouldn't have made a joke out of it. Your life *isn't* boring. But we should all be grateful that *she* doesn't know that."

"I guess," Alex agreed reluctantly. She knew she should be relieved that she was safe, but she still felt really offended by what Veronique had written.

"How about checking me out next?" Ray asked. "I'd like to see what that rat has written about me, too."

"Okay." Annie closed Alex's file, then scrolled back to Ray's and opened it. They all studied what came up on the second page of his entry:

Chances that this kid is the sought-after victim are reasonably high. He seems to be just a jerk, but he has some musical ability, a high degree of unjustified self-confidence, and reasonable intelligence. The reason he may be the person we're after is that he took an instant dislike to me and proclaimed me a fake almost as soon as he met me. Does he have telepathic abilities? Strong intuition? Or is he just naturally hard to get along with? Probability factor: 60%...

"*Jerk?*" Ray said in horror. "What a—" He was at a loss for words.

"Perceptive individual?" Annie suggested, grinning. "Come on, Ray. This is a relative of Vince's we're dealing with here. I'm willing to bet that *every* file here has nasty comments in it. She's a snake, and a chameleon. She pretends to be nice to our faces, then writes terrible things in her notes. What did you expect? A love poem?"

"No," Ray admitted. "But I think she'd make *some* comment about my great personal charm."

"Puh-lees," Annie muttered, closing his folder again. "Okay, let's try Nicole next."

Nicole's entry read as follows:

Chances that this girl could be the victim are good. She's very intelligent, remarkably well-read and eloquent, and wise beyond her years. She's also cynical, suspicious, and aggressive, all of which could have helped keep her in hiding for all of this time. On the other hand, she's apparently always been like this, so that could offset matters. Overall probability factor: 70%.

"Uh-oh," Alex muttered, worried about her friend. "It looks like Nicole's high on Veronique's list. What about Robyn?"

"Let's take a look." Annie started to scroll down the entries again, when Alex gave a start and pointed.

"Hold it, Annie," she said, and Annie stopped moving the cursor. "Right after my entry is one on *you*. And it's got an asterisk next to it."

Annie was surprised. "You're right," she agreed. "But why am I included in this? I wasn't even in your school when the accident happened." She opened the file, and they all bent forward to study the report:

Chances of this person being the accident victim are very high. Annie Mack demonstrates unusual mental abilities, bordering on genius levels—and a smugness to match. I find it hard to accept that she could have reached this plateau of intellectual thought at her age un-aided. If GC-161 enhances, then she's definitely our prime candidate.

Also suspicious is the fact that she has taken an internship at the chemical plant. This could well be a thinly disguised cover for her so that she can gather information on GC-161 for her own purposes.

On the negative side, she doesn't attend Danielle Atron Junior High, which would mean that the chances of her being the victim should therefore be low. However, her kid sis-ter *does* attend the school. Maybe Annie Mack was visiting her there? Despite this seeming contradiction in evidence, this subject is still my first choice.

Overall probability factor: 95%.

Alex felt her mouth go dry and her heart race. "Annie." She gasped. "Veronique thinks *you're* the GC-161 kid! It's *you* she's after, not *me!*"

"Yes, Alex," Annie answered, trying to sound sarcastic, as usual. But her voice sounded very, very worried. "I can see that. The question is— what do we do about it now?"

CHAPTER 10

"What have you got to worry about?" Ray asked with a shrug. "You're not the right kid, and they're bound to discover that."

Annie glared at him, her fear showing through her sarcasm. "Before or after they've finished testing me?" she asked. "Ray, I may not be in much shape to survive the tests they could subject me to. Nobody outside this room knows anything at all about the effects that GC-161 has on a human body. They're bound to subject me to all kinds of crazy tests—and when none of them work, then they'll just assume that they have to look harder. And that means *harder* on me."

"Annie's right, Ray," Alex agreed. She had been worried about herself earlier; now she discovered that she was just as scared for her sister. She and Annie didn't always get along, but she loved her sister—and knew that the feeling was mutual. She *wouldn't* let anyone hurt Annie, even if it meant that she'd have to confess to being the target of the hunt. "Can't we just erase all of that?" she asked, pointing to the computer screen.

"What's the point?" Annie replied. "Veronique still has the information, and if it disappears from her computer, then she'll start to get really suspicious."

"Well, what can we do then?" Alex asked. "We have to do *something*."

"Right," Ray agreed. "Why don't we just tell your parents what we've discovered? They're bound to throw Veronique—or whoever she really is—out of the house."

"That wouldn't solve anything, Ray," Annie pointed out patiently. "Veronique still has her files, and if we exposed her, she'd most likely be sure she's on the right track."

Alex managed a weak grin. "What we have to do," she said slowly, "is to make sure that even if she tells anybody, nobody will believe her."

Annie's face lit up. "Yes, that's *exactly* right. If everyone thinks she's unreliable, then they'll ignore whatever she says. So, we have to somehow make her look bad. Make people suspect that she doesn't know what she's talking about . . ." Then a great idea obviously hit her, because she beamed. "Or, better still, make her look *good* . . ."

Alex scowled. "I don't get it. How will that help you?"

Annie was on a roll now. "This kid is a spy, right, sent to discover who the GC-161 kid is? Well, what if we make her look like that's not the *only* thing she's after?" Annie thought furiously for a minute and then nodded in satisfaction. "Okay, Alex, we're going to need you to do some slightly delicate work. Ray, you've got a job to do, too. Between us, we're going to make Veronique look like the best spy since James Bond. . . ."

When Annie had finished outlining her plan, even Ray had to admit it was the work of a genius. Then it was time to start putting it into motion. The first thing was to return Veronique's laptop. Ray volunteered to do that, while Alex had to return the stolen wig to the bathroom. Alex picked it up, and she and Ray walked down the hall together. Leaning their ears against the bathroom door, they could hear the sounds of things being thrown about inside.

"Guess she's noticed it's missing," Ray whispered with a wide grin.

"Sounds like it," Alex agreed. "Right, off you go. It's sneaky time again."

"I can do sneaky," Ray replied happily. "All clear, Alex."

Nodding, Alex morphed into her liquid state again, taking the wig with her. Then she extruded a small part of herself under the bathroom door, so that she could see what Veronique was up to.

The visitor was dressed only in a towel and was scrambling frantically about the bathroom, looking high and low for her missing wig. She'd even started to hunt through the laundry basket. While her back was turned to the door, Alex slipped into the bathroom quickly and headed for the basket. Once inside, she re-formed, curling herself into a tight little ball. She stuffed the wig under a towel and quickly morphed again.

Alex scuttled back under the door, to safety, where she re-formed. Sooner or later, Veronique would check the laundry basket again and find the wig. She was bound to assume that she'd somehow dumped her clothes onto it and overlooked it.

Unable to restrain herself, Alex tapped on the door. "Veronique," she called, pretending to be worried. "Are you all right? I heard some noise in there."

Immediately the sounds of frantic searching stopped. "Er, yes, I am fine, Alex," the other girl called back. "I have just misplaced something, that is all."

"Would you like me to help you look for it?" Alex offered, grinning like crazy.

"No!" Veronique sounded frantic. "Er, I mean, no, it's not necessary, Alex. I have just found it."

Alex could tell that the other girl was lying. "Oh, well, I'll see you soon, then." She went back to her room, fighting the urge to laugh out loud. It had been fun teasing Veronique, and just the start of payback time. "Mission accomplished," she reported to Annie.

"Right." Annie had finished her part of the work on her computer. "I've transformed all of her files to this disc." She tapped a small floppy disc with her fingers. "As soon as I get to the chemical plant tomorrow, I can do the rest."

Alex nodded. "Time to talk to Dad, then." She gave her sister a concerned look. "Are you sure that this is going to work, Annie? I'm really worried about what might happen to you if it doesn't."

"I know you are." Annie gave her a big hug.

"I really appreciate that, Alex. But trust me—when do my ideas *ever* fail?"

"Pretty rarely," Alex admitted.

"So I've a great track record. I won't mess up on this, believe you me. Especially since my skin is riding on it." She led the way downstairs, where they found their father reading the newspaper. Ray had just reentered the room, giving the girls a quick grin and a nod to let them know he'd managed to replace the laptop. Annie nodded.

"Dad," she said, gently easing down the newspaper, so that he could see the three of them. "Can we have a word with you?"

Mr. Mack looked from his daughters to Ray. "Uh-oh," he said, smiling slightly. "You're ganging up on me. Must be something important."

"We're not ganging up on you," Annie replied. "It's just that Alex had an idea that we wanted to talk to you about, that's all."

Her father folded the newspaper and put it down. "Well, if it takes all three of you, it must be a pretty big idea. What is it?"

"Well," Alex replied, playing her enthusiastic role to the hilt, "I was thinking that we should take Veronique somewhere this weekend. I mean, she's new to America, and we should take the opportunity to show her around, shouldn't we? So she can see what life over here is like."

"Well, that sounds like a very good idea, Alex," her father agreed. "Did you have any-where in particular in mind?"

"How about the state park?" Alex suggested. "There's lots to do outdoors there—camping, climbing, canoeing . . ."

"Well, if you *really* think she'd like that," he said cheerfully.

"Oh, no," Ray butted in. "She could go to a park anytime, and pretty much anywhere in the country. You should take her somewhere special, somewhere she'll always remember. Somewhere that only Paradise Valley has."

"And where would that be, Ray?"

"The chemical plant," Ray finished with a grin. "It's the most sophisticated one in the world, and you know it like the back of your hand. Maybe even better. She could see stuff there she'd *never* see anywhere else."

"The plant?" Annie managed to sound very irritated, even though she was only acting. "Ray, that would be *boring* for her."

"It's not boring for you," Ray pointed out.

"That's because I'm an intern there," Annie objected. "It's a *job*. Why would anyone want to visit the stupid plant?"

"Now, hold on there, Annie," Mr. Mack said, thinking. "Ray does have a point. The chemical plant is the most important one of its kind in the world. Veronique would have the chance to view something completely unique."

"She'd only find it boring," Annie argued. "Alex, tell him."

"I don't know," Alex said. "She does kind of like the science classes. And she *did* ask Dad about his work there, so she *must* have some interest in the place, right?"

Annie managed to look very worried. "Yes, that's right—she *was* asking questions about the place. Maybe *too many* questions. What if she's a security risk? Dad might get her into trouble if he brought her there."

"Security risk?" Alex asked, laughing. "Honestly, you're sounding almost as bad as Ray. She's just a teenager, Annie—not James Bond."

"I do think you're overreacting," Mr. Mack agreed, staring in concern at his older daughter. "Are you sure there's not some other reason you don't want me to take Veronique to the plant?"

"No, of course not," Annie replied. Alex couldn't help but admire her sister's acting skills. She really sounded like she was worried. "It's just that . . . well, I was kind of hoping that you and I could go over your findings on GC-161 this weekend, and we could hardly do that with Veronique around, could we?"

Alex snuck a glance in the wall mirror and saw to her satisfaction that Veronique was at the top of the stairs, listening to all of this conversation. Perfect! She *had* to think that Annie was trying to hide something!

"Well, it's commendable of you to take such an interest in my work, Annie," Mr. Mack answered, patting her hand. "But we do have a responsibility to our guest, after all." He glanced up. "Ah—here's Veronique now," he said cheerily. "Well, we can ask her for her opinion."

The "exchange student" came into the room smelling of powder. She was dressed in a T-shirt and shorts, and she was wearing her blond wig once again.

"My opinion," Veronique asked, pretending she didn't know what was going on. "About what, *Monsieur* Mack?"

"Alex thought you might like to go on a trip tomorrow, while you're out of school," Mr. Mack answered. "We were thinking about the plant, but Annie thought—"

"That you'd find it *much* too dull," Annie interrupted urgently. "You'd really hate it, wouldn't you?"

"Oh, no," Veronique said innocently. "I would

love to see where you work. It sounds like a delightful idea to me."

"Well, there we are, then," Mr. Mack said firmly. "I'll just call security and arrange for passes for Veronique and Alex. And Ray, if you'd like to come along."

Ray grinned. "Trust me, I wouldn't miss this for the world," he replied.

"Excellent. So it's settled then." He beamed at Annie, who was managing to look furiously unhappy. "Cheer up, Annie. I'm sure we'll all have fun. And you and I can talk about *you-know-what* next weekend, all right?"

"I suppose so," Annie said ungraciously. "I'm going to my room now." She stormed upstairs, giving every appearance of being annoyed.

"I wonder what got into her?" Mr. Mack asked, puzzled. He looked at Alex. "She's not normally like that."

Alex shrugged. "I guess she's just feeling jealous," she suggested. "You know how special she likes to feel. She probably doesn't want all of us poking around where she works."

"Maybe you're right." Mr. Mack smiled. "Well, I'm sure she'll be a lot happier tomorrow morning. I'll just make those arrangements now."

Veronique nodded. "And I should just like to

take a *petite* walk, if you don't mind. I need to do a little thinking."

"Want me to come with you?" Alex offered.

"Oh, no," Veronique said hastily. "I just wish to be alone and think a little."

"Okay." Alex had been pretty sure she wouldn't be invited along. "I guess I'll go upstairs and watch a little TV then. Good night, Ray."

"See you bright and early," Ray promised, waving his farewell. As Mr. Mack went into the den to phone, Veronique slipped out of the front door. Alex, feeling very confident, dashed upstairs.

"You were terrific!" she enthused to Annie.

Annie grinned back. "I was, wasn't I?" she agreed. "Veronique has *got* to be convinced that I didn't want her around because I want some background on GC-161 to help me with my . . . problem."

"And she's just gone running off outside," Alex informed her. "I wonder why that could possibly be?" Then she and Annie broke out giggling, knowing full well where Veronique had to be heading right this minute.

The phone-company van was parked a block away from where it had been the last time. Veronique tapped on the rear door and then jumped inside. Her Uncle Vince stared hard at her.

"Good news," she informed him. "The Macks are taking me to the chemical plant tomorrow. Annie seemed *very* nervous with this, and tried very hard to stop her father taking me. Luckily, his idiot kid, Alex, and that dumb-dumb Ray Alvarado convinced him to ignore her."

"So you think that this Annie Mack is the GC-161 kid, then?" Vince asked, scowling.

"She's got to be," Veronique insisted. "She fits almost entirely into the pattern."

Vince nodded thoughtfully. "And when a couple of my other plans to expose the kid broke down," he mused, "she *was* always around." He thought for a moment. "Okay, Vincie, I'll back your work here. I'll call Ms. Atron tonight. I know she'll want to be there when we put the cuffs on this kid. And if you're right, I'll get reinstated, and you'll get a nice reward."

"I can hardly wait," Veronique answered, rubbing her hands greedily together. "I know I'm right."

"You'd better be," Vince replied. "Because if you're wrong, and Annie Mack *isn't* the GC-161 kid, then I'll be humiliated, and you'll be on the next plane to Nome, Alaska. Got it?"

Veronique nodded. "There's no need to sound

so worried, Uncle. I guarantee that we'll have the right kid in that factory tomorrow. Then it'll be up to you to make sure you can capture her."

Vince took a small device from one of his shelves. "I can manage that without any problem," he promised. "This is a GC-161 detector. It will show whether any of the chemical has been absorbed into Annie Mack's bloodstream." He grinned. "Tomorrow, we're going to have us a fresh captive . . ."

CHAPTER 11

Vince had almost forgotten how ice-cold Ms. Atron's eyes could be until she turned them on him once again. She was dressed impeccably, as always, without a hair out of place. She gave the impression of absolute self-confidence. More than the impression, in fact—she believed in her own abilities utterly.

"This had better not be another one your fiascos, Vince," she informed him. "You've been promising me the target child for two years now and have always failed to deliver."

Vince winced at the rebuke, knowing that it was at least partially justified. "Well, this time it won't be," he answered, trying to match her confidence. "I've had an agent planted in the

school to gather information for me. We've ze-
roed in on one special individual, and you're
going to have her in your hands today. In fact"—
he tried to sound casual—"you've had her in
your hands quite a few times already."

Danielle Atron glared icily at him. "I don't
have the time or the patience for riddles, Vince.
What are you talking about?"

"Her name is Annie Mack," Vince explained.
"And she's an intern here at the plant. I believe
she's been using that position to delve into our—
your research into GC-161."

Ms. Atron raised a plucked eyebrow. "Really?
An interesting theory. But I trust that you have
proof?"

"That's the purpose of this little trip here
today," Vince informed her. "My agent will expose the girl, and we will have our victim." He
tossed the GC-161 detector he was carrying from
palm to palm. "This little device will do the
rest."

"Well," Ms. Atron said after a moment's consideration, "if this works, Vince, you will certainly have your old job back—and a tidy bonus,
as well."

"Thank you, Ms. Atron," Vince said, genu-
inely pleased.

"And if it fails," she continued in the same

pleasant tones, "I shall take great pleasure in having you thrown bodily off the premises." She smiled coldly at him. "Just so we understand each other."

"Of course." Vince's eyes hooded at the thought of further humiliation. But what did he have to be worried about? This was bound to work.

He was *almost* certain. . . .

Mr. Mack drew the family car to a halt at the first security barrier. "Well, kids, here we are," he announced. "Of course, you know that, don't you, Annie, since you work here, too? Well, the rest of you—"

"We get the picture, Dad," Alex said gently, to cut off a rerun. "We're here."

"Right." Mr. Mack smiled as he showed his pass to the guard at the gate. "Now, everybody show your passes. Security procedures, you know."

Dutifully, Annie, Alex, Veronique, and Ray held up their passes for the guard to examine. Veronique clutched her laptop in her free hand. As Annie had planned, the spy had brought it along with her. Alex smiled. *So far, so good.*

Of course, the complicated part of the plan was still to come. Annie had made her go over it three times this morning already, insisting that they couldn't afford any mistakes. Alex knew that, but she had had a hard time concentrating after the second run-through.

"Right," Mr. Mack said brightly. "Here we go." The barrier in front of them rose, and he drove slowly down the roadway toward the main building. Since it was a Saturday, there weren't too many cars parked here, and they had plenty of options for a parking space. Mr. Mack took one about ten spaces away from a large jet-black sedan with tinted windows. The license plate read simply ATRON. Alex smiled again. Ms. Atron was here, which meant that Vince must have convinced her that something was going to happen.

Something was—but hopefully not what Vince was planning. . . .

Mr. Mack led the way to the main doors, where there was another guard. "Time to show our passes again," he announced, offering his to the guard. "Sorry about this, but there are literally hundreds of companies who'd love to see what goes on in here."

Annie nudged Alex, who said, "Wow, Dad! Are you talking about industrial espionage?"

"That's right, Alex," her father agreed. "Plenty

of companies would pay a lot of money to get information on the research we're doing here."

"Think of that," Ray said cheerfully. "Stinkers, aren't they?"

Mr. Mack studied him seriously. "It's a rough world out there, Ray," he said seriously. "There are a lot of unpleasant things that happen."

"I'll be careful," Ray promised solemnly, but there was a twinkle of amusement in his eyes. Alex understood. Her father sometimes had a tendency to state the obvious.

"Good. Okay, come along." Mr. Mack led the way into the building. "I'll take you to our publicity department first. They have lots of information brochures filled with color photos that will explain what we do here." He beamed at Veronique. "It'll make a great souvenir for you to take back to Toulon with you."

"Um, Dad," Annie said. "I'll go ahead and check that the lab's in order. You can catch up with me there. I'll set up the safe stuff for display."

"Good idea," Mr. Mack agreed. "After all, you don't need any brochures, do you? Okay, we'll see you in about ten minutes."

"No problem," Annie promised. "I'll have everything ready for you." She managed to give

Alex a big wink, then hurried off to do her part in the plan.

The publicity department was not really too interesting, but Alex managed to fake enthusiasm for the glossy magazine-style brochures her father handed out. She knew it was nothing but public relations material designed to make Paradise Valley Chemical look like the greatest invention since the CD player. There was no mention of GC-161 or the accident, naturally. No bad publicity was allowed. Veronique, too, managed to seem enthusiastic about things, and she asked a few questions that made Mr. Mack beam as he offered explanations. There was nothing he enjoyed more than enlightening people on a subject that was dear to his heart. Finally, though, he rubbed his hands together.

"Now for the really interesting part of the tour," he announced. "I shall be showing you some areas that will be marked as top secret and for authorized personnel only. You can't enter anywhere with those signs, or try to see what is there. Do you all understand?"

"Yes, Dad," Alex agreed. "We're not children. We can follow rules."

"Of course you can," her father agreed. "I just wanted to be absolutely certain, that's all."

He led them down the plushly carpeted, dark

gray corridor, past the company logos on the wall. "Progress at any cost," they read. Alex winced. Certainly, Ms. Atron placed progress above safety—and above her conscience, if she had one buried deep in her frozen heart. Then they came to her father's lab.

It was very large, very modern, and filled with equipment. Alex couldn't even begin to guess what most of it was for. Science wasn't her strong point. Annie, of course, had almost drooled when she had first walked in here. *She* knew the name and function of everything in the room, naturally. To Alex, it was like an upscale version of Dr. Frankenstein's lab.

And a room much like this was where she'd be held and probed if Ms. Atron ever found out *she* was the GC-161 kid. It made the equipment look ominous to Alex, even though she could hardly blame the machines.

Down the center of the large room were two long tables filled with computers and equipment. Annie looked up from one of the computers and smiled. "I've got the T-120 simulation ready to run, Dad," she said cheerfully. "I thought that would be a good one."

"Excellent choice, Annie," her father said approvingly. To the others, he explained: "T-120 is a new air freshener that we've developed here.

It overcomes one of the biggest problems associated with the conventional spray-can freshener. Does anyone know what that is?"

"It stinks?" Ray suggested.

Mr. Mack frowned slightly. "Well, not really. They are supposed to be scented." When nobody else had any suggestions, he informed them: "The problem is duration. They simply don't last very long, and sometimes you have to spray and respray. You see, the molecules tend to break down easily, and then have to be replaced. With T-120, the scent lasts much longer than normal thanks to a special coating we've applied on the molecular level." He led the way to the computer that Annie had primed. "On here, you'll see the representation of how the molecule works." He beamed at them. "It's in 3-D, so it's even more fascinating than normal."

Alex winced internally. It was another of her father's boring animated molecules. He loved to produce them, but Alex could never tell any of them apart. Still, it was her job to seem very enthusiastic. "Terrific," she said, with as much joy as she could muster. "You don't want to miss this, Veronique. Let's get in close."

Veronique nodded. The computer was in a crowded area of the room—as Annie had deliberately planned. To get close to the screen, they had to squash together.

"Ouch!" Ray exclaimed. "That hurt." He glanced around, rubbing his ribs. "Uh, Veronique, could you put that thing down?" He gestured to the laptop. "You're poking me with it."

"My apologies," Veronique replied, placing the laptop on the bench behind her. "It is a little crowded 'ere." Then she bent forward to watch the screen with the others.

Alex felt a tingle of excitement, knowing that their plan was working perfectly. She caught a glimpse of Annie moving in on the laptop, but didn't see anything else, because she had to "ooh" and "aah" at the rotating molecules on the screen and listen to her father's explanation of what was going on.

Meanwhile, Alex knew precisely what was going on. Using the encryption codes she'd taken from Veronique's laptop the night before, Annie had downloaded some files from the company computers here, and then formatted them to fit the laptop. While Veronique was kept distracted, Annie was plugging into the laptop and feeding in the extra files. It would only take about thirty seconds, but it was important to keep Veronique from suspecting that anything was happening.

Fortunately, Mr. Mack kept talking and showing off his animation for a full two minutes. Alex's brain felt numb from just letting his words flow over her head. Then, finally, he stopped the molecules spinning. "Well," he said cheerfully, "wasn't *that* interesting."

"It's made me consider a career in chemistry," Ray offered, winking at Alex.

"Well, that's a good thing," Mr. Mack said approvingly. "The world needs more alert chemists, Ray. It could be a very wise career move."

"If he wasn't so clumsy," Annie offered. "Maybe you should stick to the sax, Ray." She wasn't really trying to be nasty—it was just her way to let Ray and Alex know that she'd finished her part of the job.

"Well, that could be a problem," Mr. Mack agreed. "In this business, we frown upon accidents."

"But," came an icy woman's voice, "they still sometimes happen, don't they, Mack?"

Everyone spun around to stare at the doorway. Danielle Atron stood there, looking like a store mannequin—dressed beautifully, but with no expression or warmth whatsoever on her face.

"Ms. Atron!" Mr. Mack exclaimed. "It's very good to see you again. I was just showing my daughter and her friends around the plant. I do have authorization," he added quickly, lest she think he was simply acting on a whim.

"I know you do," Ms. Atron agreed, moving into the room. "I signed it myself." Behind her came Vince, looking very smug and carrying a small piece of equipment in his hand. "I have my own reasons for wanting you here today." She glanced around at Vince. "Go on."

"It'll be a pleasure, Ms. Atron." He moved forward, a predatory gleam in his eye. Alex felt a twinge of fear, knowing that he meant exactly what he said. He was planning on exposing and capturing Annie—and he'd take a great deal of pleasure from doing so. Especially if she resisted. Vince was, essentially, a major-league bully. "This isn't going to hurt," he promised. "Yet." He held out the device he was carrying.

"What is that thing?" Alex asked. She didn't have to work at sounding scared. Just the sight of Vince was enough to give her the creeps. And when he had that nasty smile on his face, she got a major case of the shudders.

"Relax," Vince told her. "It's not for you. It's for your sister." He pushed past Alex and held the detector up in front of Annie. "Hold still, little girl."

"I am *not* a little girl," Annie said, annoyed. "And get that thing out of my face before I sue."

"It'll just take a second," Vince promised, scanning her with the device. "I have to be very close for this to register."

Then his face fell, and he stared at the readout, unable to believe his eyes. "Negative," he croaked.

"What *is* that thing?" Annie demanded, scowling at him.

"Yes," Mr. Mack added, taking a step forward and looking very concerned. "What are you doing to my daughter?"

"Nothing!" Vince said hastily. "This thing must need recalibrating." He began to fumble with the controls.

"Perhaps you'd be good enough to explain this, Ms. Atron?" Mr. Mack said firmly. "I'd like to know why Vince is harassing my daughter."

"So would I," Ms. Atron replied, her voice sounding chillier than the wind off an iceberg. Alex used this opportunity to move beside her father. It looked like a show of support—which it was, partly—but it also got her farther away from Vince and his detector, just in case.

"Just a minute," Vince mumbled, his face starting to flush. "I think this detector is malfunctioning."

"Detector?" Mr. Mack echoed. "*What* are you trying to detect?"

"GC-161," Ms. Atron admitted. "Vince seems to be suffering from a delusion that your daughter had been exposed to large quantities of the substance."

"Annie?" Mr. Mack shook his head. "I assure you, Ms. Atron, I *never* allow Annie anywhere near our test samples. It's against the security regulations, and, besides, she's my daughter. I wouldn't place her life in danger by exposing her to incompletely tested materials. I don't know what possessed Vince to think that she's been exposed, but I can assure you that she has not been."

Danielle Atron moved closer to Vince. The air temperature seemed to plummet as she did so. "I tend to agree with you, Mack." She stared at Vince. "That detector isn't showing *any* results."

"But it's got to," Vince insisted, scanning Annie again—with the same negative result. "I don't understand."

"It would appear that your information was incorrect," Ms. Atron said. There was the slightest hint of lines across her forehead—which meant that she was *very* angry indeed. Alex couldn't repress her grin. Stage one was accomplished. Now it was time for stage two.

"Why did you think I'd been exposed to GC-161?" Annie asked, looking straight at Vince.

"Yes," Ms. Atron purred dangerously. "Where *did* you get such a ludicrous idea?"

Seeing only one way to escape Ms. Atron's wrath, Vince took it. He pointed to Veronique. "*She* told me."

"You?" This was a collective chorus, with Ms. Atron and Mr. Mack the only genuine gasps among them. But it was important for Alex and Annie to play ignorant.

"Who is she?" Ms. Atron asked. "Apart from a buffoon, that is?"

Veronique saved Vince the trouble of explaining. Giving him a filthy look for betraying her, she stepped forward, clutching her laptop eagerly. "I'm his niece," she admitted, completely dropping the fake French accent. "Vincie." She whipped off her wig.

"I *knew* she was a fake," Ray said smugly.

"Gee," Alex said, still grinning, "I guess I owe you an apology, Ray. I never suspected for a second."

"You can pay me back later," Ray said generously.

"Well, young lady," Ms. Atron said, staring down at her as if she were a giant cockroach. "Perhaps *you* can explain this fiasco?"

Vincie opened the laptop and switched it on. "I've been analyzing the kids in the local school," she explained, "to determine who was the GC-161 accident victim."

Mr. Mack frowned. "But that was just an unsubstantiated rumor," he complained. "Wasn't it?" he asked Ms. Atron.

"Of course it was," she assured him smoothly. "I think Vince and his niece have flipped their lids."

"It's all here," Vincie insisted, gesturing to her laptop, which showed the icons for all of her files. Everyone crowded around as Vincie feverishly tapped the keys.

Now. Alex leaned forward, covered by the others, and touched the case of the computer. Unnoticed, she managed to send a carefully prepared zap into the device. Annie had cautioned her not to make it too powerful, and Alex had practiced hard to get it just right.

The computer began to flash, and several fresh icons popped into existence.

"Hello," Mr. Mack said, fascinated. "It looks like you've had a power surge that's opened some of your hidden files." His voice trailed off as he saw one of them. "GC-161 file Omega," he said.

"File Omega?" Ms. Atron snapped to attention. "Impossible. That file is top secret. Mack, check it out."

Mr. Mack did so, tapping in a command on the laptop. "It's encrypted," he said.

Ms. Atron turned her frozen eyes onto Vincie. "Open it."

"But—but—" Vincie stammered. "That's not one of my files. I swear!"

"Then it won't open when you put in your password, will it?" Ms. Atron pointed out. "Open it."

There was no denying her when she was in this mood. Vincie tapped in her password.

The file opened.

Mr. Mack's eyes went wide. "It *is* the Omega file." He gasped as he scanned the scientific data it contained. Alex couldn't understand any of it. "But what is it doing on . . ." Mr. Mack said, puzzled. He suddenly clicked on the answer. "She's an industrial spy!" he exclaimed, remembering his earlier conversation with Alex. "That's why she's really here. She must be concocting these charges against Annie to throw us off her track while she escapes with this information."

"Indeed." It was quite clear that Ms. Atron believed exactly the same thing. She turned to Vince. "Was *this* what you planned?" she demanded. "Stealing *my* secrets for revenge for being fired?"

"No!" he exclaimed, obviously worried and

129

scared. "I swear! I had nothing to do with that file being there. It must have been Vincie! She must be trying to go solo with this stuff. Sell it to the highest bidder."

"No!" Vincie insisted. "I've never seen that file before, honest!"

Ms. Atron turned to glare coldly at her. "You wouldn't know what honesty was if it bit you on the hand," she snapped. "Mack, erase that material—now!"

"Erasing, Ms. Atron," Alex's father said, his fingers flying over the keys.

"You," Ms. Atron said to Vince. "Get out of here. Now. And take this . . . failed *spy* with you. If you're still in the building in thirty seconds, I'll have the guards toss you out. And not gently."

Vince—furious, embarrassed, and worried— nodded hastily. "Going, Ms. Atron," he croaked. As Vincie started to protest again, he grabbed her by one ear. "Come on!" he yelled, ignoring her howl of pain. "You've got a plane to catch. To Nome." He had obviously forgotten about the laptop, which lay where Veronique had placed it.

Annie laughed. "Send us a postcard!" she called out as they left the room.

Mr. Mack straightened up. "Whew!" he exclaimed. "That was close. I erased the complete memory, Ms. Atron. That machine is now clean."

"Good." Ms. Atron almost managed to crack a smile. "Good work, Mack. You've probably saved our company a lot of money, exposing that spy."

"Oh, well, it was nothing," Mr. Mack said modestly.

Which, Alex reflected, *is absolutely true.* He'd done nothing. Still, she, Annie, and Ray couldn't take any credit without getting into a lot of explanations.

"I won't be ungrateful," Ms. Atron informed him, heading toward the door. "Look for a little thank-you in your next paycheck."

Mr. Mack's eyebrows rose. "Thank you, Ms. Atron!" he called to her retreating back. Then he turned back to his daughters and Ray. "Well!" he exclaimed. "That was quite exciting. And *very* unexpected. Fancy Veronique actually being a spy. And she stayed with us all of this time and we never suspected a thing."

"I did," Ray said smugly. "I had her pegged as a fake from the start. Only nobody would believe me."

Annie put an arm around his shoulder. "Well, we'll know better from now on, won't we?" she asked, grinning.

"Right," Alex agreed, putting her arms around both her sister and her friend. As her father went off to turn off the computer they'd been studying earlier, Alex lowered her voice. "Thanks, guys," she murmured. "We did it."

"Yes," Annie agreed, obviously very pleased with herself. "You're off the hook again. And so am I." She raised an eyebrow. "You did that zap beautifully, Alex."

Alex grinned. "Thank you. Things are looking up. We've got rid of Veronique, and Dad's managed to solve my music problem. Monday morning, I bet you I blow the other musicians away."

Mr. Mack hurried back. "Well," he said, still looking a little puzzled. "I think that ends the tour for today. What do you all say to stopping off at the mall on the way home, and I'll buy everyone lunch?"

"Sounds great to me," Annie said enthusiastically. "I'm starving."

"Count us in, too," Alex agreed. "Only—no veggie burgers, okay?"

"The real thing," her father promised.

Alex nodded happily. Despite everything, things had turned out just fine after all. It was the start of a grand weekend. And on Monday, she'd play "St. Patrick's Day" on her tin whistle for Miss Henderson. She *knew* she'd get the extra credit.

As they left the room, Alex couldn't resist sending one last zap back at the laptop, frying all its circuits. "So there," she murmured. No way now would *anything* in that machine be used against anyone.

"Come on, Alex!" her father called.

"Coming!" she replied, and hurried to catch up with three of her favorite people in the world.

About the Author

JOHN PEEL was born in Nottingham, England—home of Robin Hood. He moved to the United States in 1981 to get married and now lives on Long Island with his wife, Nan, their wire-haired fox terrier, Dashiell, and their feline terror, Amika. He has written more than sixty books, including novels based on the top British science fiction TV series, *Doctor Who*, and the top American science fiction TV series, *Star Trek*. He has written several supernatural thrillers for young adults that are published by Archway Paperbacks—*Talons*, *Shattered*, *Poison*, and *Maniac*. *Star Trek: Deep Space Nine: Prisoners of Peace* and *Field Trip* are available from Minstrel Books.

John has written several Nickelodeon titles for the *Are You Afraid of the Dark?* series: *The Tale of the Sinister Statues*, *The Tale of the Restless House*, *The Tale of the Zero Hero*, and *The Tale of the Three Wishes*.